Jordan
Stryker

Jordan Stryker
CYBER TERROR

MALCOLM ROSE

USBORNE

With thanks to Nathan Fenwick for his enthusiasm and to Lemon Jelly for the song, "Ramblin' Man".

First published in the UK in 2011 by Usborne Publishing Ltd., Usborne House, 83-85 Saffron Hill, London EC1N 8RT, England. www.usborne.com

Copyright © Malcolm Rose, 2011

The right of Malcolm Rose to be identified as the author of this work has been asserted by him in accordance with the Copyright, Designs and Patents Act, 1988.

Cover illustration by Daniel Atanasov at folioart.co.uk

The name Usborne and the devices ♈ ⊕ are Trade Marks of Usborne Publishing Ltd.

This is a work of fiction. The characters, incidents, and dialogues are products of the author's imagination and are not to be construed as real. Any resemblance to actual events or persons, living or dead, is entirely coincidental.

A CIP catalogue record for this book is available from the British Library.

ISBN 9781409509776 J MAMJJASOND/11 01770/1

Printed in Reading, Berkshire, UK.

1 FLIGHT DOWN

Flight LH6681 bound for Heathrow was carrying 138 passengers and crew when it took off from Edinburgh Airport at 15.05 on Monday 5th March. The pilot was Phil Lazenby, the weather was fine and the first three minutes of the journey were smooth.

Control: "LH six-six-eight-one, you're cleared to turn right, heading two-four-zero."

Pilot: "Affirm turning two-four-zero. Climbing to cruising altitude. Thanks."

Control: "Bon voyage. Over and out."

Pilot: "Hang on. Control? Stay with me."

Control: "I'm all ears. What's wrong?"

Pilot: "Something's... Just a second."

Control: "Report, please, LH six-six-eight-one."

Pilot: "Yes. We've lost thrust in both engines."

Control: "What? Say again."

Pilot: "Major electronic fault. We've lost thrust in both engines. Turning back to airport."

Control: "Okay. Do you want to land main runway?"

Pilot: "Descending rapidly. Probably unable to circle to main runway. Heading for secondary runway."

Control: "Tower stopping all departures and arrivals for emergency return."

There were a few seconds of radio silence. Uncannily quiet, the powerless Airbus 320 banked and plunged towards the earth.

Control: "Secondary runway confirmed clear, LH six-six-eight-one. We can accommodate you. Repeat. You have permission for emergency landing on secondary runway."

The co-pilot had just passed the training course to fly an Airbus. The journey to Edinburgh and back to London was Toby Cotterill's first outing. He was monitoring all onboard flight components. With a look of horror on his face, he was watching them all go down, one after the other. His training required him to remain calm. He was no use to the pilot – or to the passengers – if he panicked. But keeping cool was difficult when his heart was pounding like crazy, the plane had just become a giant glider and the rest of his life might be measured in minutes. His time was ticking down to zero just like the altimeter. He glanced across at the pilot and said, "The landing gear's out of action as well. It won't budge."

"Activate the auxiliary power unit."

"No effect."

"Deploy the ram air turbine, then," the captain said.

"Nothing happening. We've got basic power – radio, lights and such – but the flight system isn't responding. It's dead."

"No engines and no landing gear." Keeping the plane's nose up as much as possible, Captain Lazenby swore under his breath. Yet he was also determined and decisive. "Change of plan. I'm bringing her down in the Firth of Forth."

Toby swallowed. "What?"

"Have you got a better idea?"

"No," he admitted.

"Coming down on water, at least we don't risk the lives of people on the ground."

The co-pilot nodded. "Agreed."

The cockpit door opened. The chief steward gasped, "What's happening? What's with the engines? The passengers are panicking."

"The flight system's failed," Toby told her. "Get them to brace for impact. We're going down on the water."

"Right." A quake of the voice gave away the flight attendant's feelings. Even so, she snapped into action and went back to her passengers.

"Did you copy that, Control?" the pilot asked. "We're ditching in the river."

"It's your call, LH six-six-eight-one."

"We're going to need boats – and plenty of them. Scramble emergency services."

"Understood. Whereabouts in the river?"

"Unable to plot exact course," Captain Lazenby replied, guiding the jet with manual controls. "But they'll see the splash."

Captain Lazenby knew that almost all planes broke up when they struck water. There was only one angle to hit the river without shattering the aircraft. It was like skimming a stone across a lake or a spacecraft re-entering the atmosphere. It had to be precise to be successful. But he had little control over navigation and he had only one chance.

Toby Cotterill was going through the emergency procedure checklist in an attempt to restart the engines. Without a working control system, though, his effort would be wasted.

"What about the ditch switch?" Captain Lazenby asked. It was the device for sealing all vents and valves in the fuselage to make the plane less likely to flood, more likely to float.

The co-pilot shook his head. "No response."

To the captain's left were four golf courses and the north-west sector of Edinburgh. On the right was the green countryside around Barnbougle Castle. Straight ahead was the Firth of Forth, as flat as a landing strip.

A voice from the ground said, "I've cleared all traffic in controlled airspace. Overflights only. You've got it to yourself."

"Affirm. Copied information." Captain Lazenby looked across briefly at Toby. Sky high on adrenalin, he said, "Let's do it. Banking left. I'm going in close to South Queensferry – as near to the bridges as possible. Less distance for rescuers."

Phil breathed deeply, composing himself. He judged that he was too low and too slow but, now that he was piloting a glider rather than a jet aeroplane, there was little he could do about it.

Control asked, "What's your status, LH six-six-eight-one?"

The pilot ran his eye over the cockpit controls and Toby shook his head. "Flight system still dead."

"Emergency services scrambled. I'll have them standing by at Queensferry."

"In case I bring this down in one piece, Control, you'd better have a whisky on standby as well."

"I'm a bit busy at the moment, LH six-six-eight-one, but I'll see what I can do."

The co-pilot grimaced, making it clear that he didn't think it was the right time to share a joke with air traffic control.

Given what he was about to do, Captain Lazenby needed a smile on his face. He'd abandoned the usual flight path and the Firth of Forth was rushing towards him. The silent Airbus tilted as he turned tightly so that the railway bridge was directly ahead. He veered towards the southern bank of the estuary so the Airbus would ditch nearer to land.

"Too steep," he muttered to himself, trying to keep

the nose of the plane pointing upwards.

But the water seemed to draw the plane in.

"Is that a ferry I see in the river?"

Control replied, "If it is, it'll probably be the Rosyth to Zeebrugge. Is it in your way?"

Captain Lazenby's voice sounded tired, as if he were talking at the same time as running a marathon. "No. Make contact. Keep it where it is on standby."

The river sped underneath the cockpit like a flash flood. Wind buffeted the Airbus and its right wing touched the surface of the water. The aeroplane juddered and jerked. Luggage shifted around the cargo hold, upsetting the plane's balance even more. The pilots and passengers were pummelled in their seats.

A few seconds more and their ordeal would be over. One way or another.

Phil Lazenby steadied himself – steadied the plane – and let it drop into the Firth of Forth.

The Airbus had been in the air for six minutes and forty-six seconds when it hit the water at 220 kilometres per hour. It didn't bounce like a flat stone. It slammed into the water like a log ride hurtling down a water chute. There was a huge splash. For a moment, spray completely covered the plane. Phil was pitched forward awkwardly until his seat belt dislocated his shoulder. The jolt tore the plane's underbelly and peeled off much of its aluminium skin, making large gashes in the bottom of the fuselage. At the rear, the cargo doors were wrenched open. The impact also broke three windows. Water flooded in through the holes. Within seconds, the passengers and crew were up to their knees in cold river water.

When the plane came to a standstill, the cabin was quiet, apart from the sound of passengers crying, praying and talking urgently on mobiles. Then the flight attendants began to shout orders. Making sure everyone had got into their yellow life-jackets, they ushered people out of the mid-cabin emergency exits above the wings and evacuated passengers near the front down the two inflatable chutes. They gave most help to the injured and women with children as the water level rose to their waists.

Strangely, there was no sense of panic. Everyone was unnaturally calm. They were probably in shock. By the time the flight attendants were ready to leave the plane and Captain Lazenby had waded laboriously up and down the aisle, to make sure he was the last person on board, the water was at chest height.

The Airbus was submerged up to its windows and it was sinking slowly, but it seemed determined to stay afloat until everyone had been rescued. Its tail fin poking up out of the water, it was drifting eastwards on the lazy river current.

138 people were huddled together in groups, standing on the wings or the partially submerged chutes. A few passengers had slipped off the wings and into the water. Or perhaps, fearing that the plane was about to sink or explode, they'd decided to swim for the shore.

A ferry, several pleasure boats and a couple of rescue craft made their way to the stricken aeroplane within three minutes of the crash landing. Amateurs and professionals alike plucked stranded passengers from the wings, the water and the chutes which had detached from the aircraft to form life-rafts. The coming and going of boats continued until all of the passengers and aircrew of Flight LH6681 were safely back on land.

Under the circumstances, the toll of injuries was light: one heart attack, four head wounds, several cases of exposure among those dragged from the water, one serious laceration to the arm, a broken leg and a dislocated shoulder. The flashbacks, panic attacks and sleeplessness would hit many of them later.

The waterlogged Airbus was towed to Leith Docks and moored there while the on-scene investigation began.

2 MUCH MODIFIED

Waiting for the traffic lights in Highgate Village to turn green, Jordan Stryker looked up. For some reason, he wondered if he could punch his way out through the top of his car in an emergency. He didn't know. He couldn't do it with his left fist. He didn't have to attempt it to know that the reinforced metal roof would be too strong for flesh and bone. He didn't yet have the same instinct for his false right arm. He knew that, if he shoved it out of the window of the moving car and let it slam into a concrete lamp post, his bionic arm would come off worse. If he walloped a pedestrian or cyclist, he'd damage the person more than the robotic gadget attached to his right shoulder. But he hadn't yet worked out his limitations. He might be able to smash through the roof and he might not.

The lights changed and Jordan accelerated.

Straight away, a police officer on a motorbike indicated that he should pull over and stop. The policeman took off his helmet and strolled up to Jordan's jet black Jaguar. "Get out," he demanded.

Jordan sighed and did as he was told.

The traffic cop looked him up and down with an expression of disdain on his face. "You're young." He seemed to have decided already that Jordan had committed a driving offence. A teenager in a flash car was all the evidence he appeared to need. "Your licence, please." Then he smirked and added, "As if you've got one."

"Yes, I've got one," Jordan replied calmly.

Jordan Stryker was fourteen, but the date of birth shown on his driving licence made him seventeen years old. He was a much modified boy with a modified ID, driving a much modified Jaguar XJ Sentinel.

More than a year before, an explosion had wiped out

his immediate family and almost destroyed him. An underground organization called Unit Red had taken care of him, rebuilt his broken body and given him a new identity. Now, Jordan was part human and part machine. He had a robotic right arm, brain implants that gave him acute hearing, a fantastic sense of smell and a connection to the internet, as well as bionic eyes with a range of wavelengths. Whenever he wanted, he could turn on his night vision or the terahertz technology that allowed him to see through material. He used his enhancements as an agent for Unit Red, tackling the bad guys who were beyond normal law. It was also Unit Red that had given him his car and driving licence.

The police officer examined the licence, stared at Jordan and then studied the card again. Plainly, he was struggling to believe the first four digits of Jordan's licence number. They formed a code that told him Jordan was not to be hindered. "This means..."

Jordan nodded. "Let's not talk about it here. I didn't nick the car and I'm not a joyrider. Despite appearances. I need to get going."

"Right." The traffic cop returned the licence and muttered, "Sorry to...you know."

"No problem," Jordan replied with a cheeky smile.

He started the engine again and turned into Swain's

Lane. He could set the electric car to run in silent mode, but it had an electronic sound generator wired into its motor. The gadget monitored the revs and produced a synthetic engine noise, modelled on the powerful purr of a supercharged V8 engine. It alerted pedestrians to the car's presence.

Jordan let the Jaguar roll down the hill to Unit Red's headquarters in Highgate Cemetery and halted by the locked garage doors. Using one of his brain implants, he thought the password into the on-board computer. At once, the car transmitted the electronic key to the garage door and it eased open. Jordan steered the car slowly up to its recharging point in the engineering workshop and the door slid down securely behind him.

He walked through the house and took the lift down to the underground rooms, heading straight to the bunker because Unit Red's boss wanted to see him.

When he entered, Angel looked up from his monitor. Even sitting, the chief looked impressively tall. He was in his late thirties, lean and self-assured. "Good," he said, seeing Jordan. "I know you were putting the car through its paces, but I ordered you back because something's come up. I've just been handed a new case. The usual agencies aren't getting anywhere, so it's come to us. I think it's one for you."

Jordan sat down opposite Angel. "Oh?"

He nodded. "You won't remember the Edinburgh Airport incident – and the pilot's heroic landing in the river – because you were still out of commission, learning to master your arm. Never mind. Basically, a plane lost all control in mid-air. You can access the details on the system." He tapped his workstation. "A month before that, there was another incident. A flight took off from Quito en route to Amsterdam. Same thing. Within minutes, an electronic fault brought it down with a full load of fuel. There wasn't much left to investigate after the explosion. And there was total loss of life."

"Quito? Where's that?"

"Ecuador." Angel continued, "In one case, an explosion and fire stopped the experts diagnosing exactly what happened. In the other, water ruined the electronics. The planes' black boxes weren't specific. Both recorded an unknown electronic fault that crashed the flight system. So, in the absence of solid evidence, what are the possibilities? How did someone knock both planes out of the sky?"

"Just a minute," Jordan said. "How do you know it was done on purpose? Maybe something just went wrong with both planes." Thinking of one of his mum's sayings, he added, "Accidents happen."

"Before Quito, whoever did it announced there'd be a disaster. He didn't say where or what type. He was making sure we knew it was deliberate. It was terrorism, not an accident. After Quito, he demanded a ransom or he'd do the same in Britain."

"So we refused to pay up and he went ahead?"

Angel shook his head. "The government wouldn't admit it publicly, but they dropped five million precisely where it was supposed to be dropped. It wasn't touched and he hit Edinburgh anyway. This isn't about money. It's someone who gets kicks out of making us squirm and pay up. When I say *someone*, I mean a man, woman or a group of people. I'll play you his sound clips in a minute. But first..."

"How he did it?"

"Yes." Angel stood up and walked up and down behind his desk. "The real answer is, we don't know. But our computer specialists have come up with three possibilities. Black-box recorders couldn't distinguish them. A cyber attack, a hardware Trojan, or an e-bomb."

Jordan looked blank. He'd heard of a cyber attack. That was a fancy name for hacking and computer viruses. He didn't have a clue about the other two.

"There's no evidence anyone hacked into the aviation

computers, but it can't be ruled out. A Trojan's harder to pin down. You'll get a full briefing later, but it's a microchip that was sabotaged with a bad circuit when it was made. It can be activated at any time, turning the microprocessor into a time bomb."

"Aren't chips tested before they get put in planes – or anywhere else?"

Angel nodded. "But there's no way of detecting a single extra circuit among millions of genuine ones on a chip. The kill switch only makes itself known when it's triggered. By then, it's too late. The chip's dead and whatever was relying on it is down and out."

"And that's called a hardware Trojan?"

"Yes. The third possibility's an electromagnetic bomb." Angel sat at his desk again. "Did you know you could down a plane, or even bring a city to its knees, in a fraction of a second without firing a single shot, spilling a drop of blood or blasting a single building? That's an e-bomb for you. It's simple to make and it doesn't leave a trace. It's a strong burst of microwaves and it'd burn out all circuits and crash every computer within a few hundred square metres."

"Does that mean it fries chips?" Jordan said, with a smile on his face.

"This is serious, Jordan."

"Yeah, I know."

"The pulse creates a power surge in circuits, like giving all electronic gear a heart attack." Angel sighed. "Cyber warfare, a hardware Trojan or an e-bomb could trash an aircraft's power and control systems at a distance. Or worse. Crippling a few planes and killing the passengers is bad enough. But we could be facing the end of civilization."

"That's a bit..."

"Extreme? Not really," Angel said. "Think about it. Society – civilization – depends on computers and technology. If someone could disrupt crucial computers, it'd be the end of everything. Energy generation and distribution. We'd have no power. Then there's pumping stations. They'd grind to a halt. That means no drinking water after half a day and no petrol or diesel transport because there'd be no pumps to refuel vehicles. No deliveries. Supermarket shelves would empty in two or three days, no supplies of drugs would get to hospitals. So, no water, no food, no medicine, no power. Emergency generators would only work till they ran out of fuel. Health care and hospital services would collapse in seventy-two hours. How long do you think we'd last after that? How long before people riot on the streets?"

"I see what you mean."

"Remember, there's no heating, no telecommunications, no internet, no emergency services. Sewage wouldn't get pumped away. Banks, stock exchanges and just about every other business would go into meltdown. The armed forces rely on communication, so they'd be out of it as well." He raised his arms in a gesture of hopelessness. "Need I go on? That's not just a spanner in the works. It's chaos and complete breakdown. Pretty much the end of civilization as far as I'm concerned. Experts tell me it'd take four to ten years to recover from an attack like that."

Jordan remembered his mum once saying that civilization is only three or four meals away from anarchy. At the time, he hadn't understood. He did now, though. "If it's such a big deal, why are you giving this job to me?" he asked.

"Because you've got an extra incentive to sort it out."

"How do you mean?"

"Society depends on technology. So do you. An e-bomb would scramble your circuits. If you've got a Trojan chip inside you, you could be crippled at the flick of a switch. Or a hacker could break into your systems and disable you. That'll spur you on, to say the least. But you won't be on your own. I'll give you all the backup you need. Now," he said, "do you want to hear him – or her? The police called him Short Circuit."

Jordan nodded and sat up attentively.

Accessing the sound file through his computer, Angel explained, "His first message – before the crash in Ecuador – was short and not very sweet. He simply announced in advance when something bad was going to happen. This was his second. Like the first, it's heavily distorted. My sound gurus tell me it's been through several stages of manipulation to disguise the voice. Before you ask, background noise has been filtered out. Apart from the sound of an aeroplane taking off and that's probably been layered over the top to remind us of the threat. It doesn't mean he lives near Gatwick or Heathrow. Or Edinburgh." Angel struck the *Enter* key to play the file.

The Quito incident was a step on the way to proving I can cripple anything. Transport, energy, banks, government, shops. If it has electronic circuitry, it is in my power. That includes the whole of society.

I hope you don't doubt my ability. That would be a big mistake. Five million pounds will go some way to encouraging me not to repeat the exercise

*on British soil. I shouldn't say British soil. That is
not accurate. The money will encourage me not to
repeat it in British sky.*

*Films are very helpful. At least, thrillers and TV
cops are. They show you the procedure for handing
over ransom money. I want five million in used
unmarked notes...*

Angel turned down the volume. "He's finished his
main rant. It goes on – in huge detail – about the
mechanics of dropping the money in Kingston..."

"Kingston?"

"Upon Thames. Surrey. Anyway, you can check it out
later, if you like. It came to nothing. He didn't pick it up."

The voice could have come out of a synthesizer. It
wasn't natural in any way. The terrorist could have been
male or female, young or old. Any accent was lost in the
distortion. It could have been an English, American,
Australasian or Canadian voice. It could have been
Scottish, Welsh or Irish.

"Have you heard from him since?" Jordan asked.

Angel nodded. He stopped the recording and set up
another. "This is the latest." He clicked on the file.

I wanted to make sure I have scared you enough

to pay whatever I ask. Actually, I think money is grubby. It's not worth worrying about. I can think of far more important things. Dignity is very important. I think it is perhaps the most important thing. Another important thing is fairness. I know what's fair and what isn't, but some people don't understand the difference. I am going to bring them down before I target everyone. They will be good practice.

The brief sound file came to a halt.

Angel said, "I'm not sure what that means, but there could be a hint of *why* he's doing it. Some sort of grievance, perhaps. Something he thinks was unfair that hurt his pride. That's one of your jobs. Find out what's behind his thinking. Then there's *how* he's doing it, who he is and – most important of all – stopping him before he steps up a gear to threatening everyone and civilization itself."

The pressure of responsibility made Jordan gulp. He wanted to protest that he was just a teenager, but he knew it was no good. In return for repairing his smashed body, Unit Red wanted something from him. It wanted an agent who did not look like an agent. It wanted him to use his powers against terrorists and crooks who had evaded justice. His debt to Unit Red was too great to walk away or to refuse a mission.

Jordan had become a spook. He'd never heard anyone in Unit Red refer to agents as spooks. Perhaps they reserved the term for their creepy neighbours in Highgate Cemetery.

He stood upright and said, "Just a couple of things. How did these voice clips turn up?"

"They were e-mailed from untraceable addresses to the police computer in Manchester."

"Manchester?"

"No one knows why. Maybe there's a reason, or he could've just stuck a pin in a map. What's your second thought?"

"Why Ecuador then Edinburgh? Why pick on those two flights?"

Angel shrugged. "It could've been random, but I doubt it. I should think there's a connection. That's a good place to start."

3 SHORT CIRCUIT

Kate Stelfox was not his handler's real name. It was an invention, like Jordan Stryker, Angel and Raven. For confidentiality, Unit Red agents were only ever known by code names.

Raven was one of the organization's electronic whizz-kids, yet she defied the geeky stereotype. In her mid-twenties, she was glamorous, slim, heavily made-up and dressed as if she were on her way to a nightclub. She filled the air with a perfume that Jordan's olfactory system identified as oranges, blackcurrant, jasmine and cedar wood. It smelled expensive. On sizeable heels, she stood in front of the wall-to-ceiling window that overlooked Highgate Cemetery's stone crosses, headstones and monuments. To Jordan and Kate, sitting next to each other on the sofa, she seemed to have an enchanted wood behind her as she briefed them.

"Have you heard of this? When a nuclear bomb goes off, you generate an electromagnetic pulse that overloads electrical systems for miles around."

Jordan shook his head, but Kate said, "Yes, I think I knew that. Probably a documentary on the telly."

"Lightning and high-energy particles from a solar storm can do it as well. They create a massive current that short circuits everything. An e-bomb has the same effect, but you don't have to fire a nuke or wait for the right weather. You can generate enough of a radio-frequency shock wave with pretty simple equipment. You could cobble it together for a few hundred quid using off-the-shelf gear from an electrical shop or the internet."

"Someone like me could do it?" Jordan asked.

"You'd need to download instructions from the net, but the components and know-how are out there, yes."

"Scary," he muttered.

"The powers-that-be are keeping quiet about it because they don't want the bad guys to know how easy it is. You don't want e-bombs in the wrong hands. But – with Edinburgh and Quito – maybe it's already happened."

Kate asked, "How big are these things? Would they fit in a pocket, like a phone, or would you need a lorry to cart one around?"

"It's between the two. About the size of a briefcase. You'd have to get it on the plane or put it on the ground within about a kilometre of the plane coming in to land or taking off. Either way, the microwave flash would be powerful enough to bring the plane down." Raven hesitated and added, "Angel asked me to put all the technical stuff on file so you can access it. Riveting bedtime reading."

"That's an e-bomb," Jordan said. "What about a hardware Trojan?"

"That's easier to get your head around," she answered. "We've got microchips everywhere these days. Faulty ones are somewhere between inconvenient and dangerous. You could be booking a train journey when the internet packs up, or you could be in a plane when the engines cut out." She paused to gather her jet-black hair and push it over her left shoulder. "We've only got ourselves to blame. We rely far too much on technology. What happens is, you spike a chip with a hidden circuit that does nothing until you send a trigger message. Then it blows the chip. Easily enough to screw up a plane's flight and control systems."

Jordan said, "What's the trigger?"

"There are a few. The only one that makes sense for attacking planes is activating the Trojan with a radio signal."

"How close would you have to get?" asked Jordan.

"I'm not sure," Raven replied. "You'd probably need to be near enough to have a direct line of sight to the target."

Kate was puzzled. "Wouldn't the chip have to be sabotaged where it's made?"

Raven nodded.

"But if someone makes a few Trojan chips," Kate said, "how does he get them where he needs them – like into a plane he wants to bring down?"

Jordan wondered if he'd already figured out the answer. He leaped in before Raven could respond. "Aren't almost all chips made by one company?"

"Yes," Raven said. "Worldwide, eighty per cent are from the same source."

"Well, if he worked there, he'd be pretty sure his chips

would get into almost everything. Planes included. He'd just have to sneak a rogue circuit into the design."

"I suppose so," Raven replied, taken aback by Jordan's quick reasoning. "The company would churn out millions of them without knowing a thing about it."

Kate nodded. "It makes sense. That way, he'd have a few sleeping Trojans in most IT systems across the planet, waiting for him to wake them up and cause havoc. What's this company?"

"HiSpec. Short for HiSpec MicroSystems."

"So," Kate suggested, "Jordan could be looking for a HiSpec worker with a whopping gripe of some sort."

"Something like that."

"Could I have some of these dodgy chips in my head and arm?" Jordan asked.

Raven nodded again. "You, the Unit Red computer network, your car, almost anything."

"Where's the HiSpec factory?" he asked.

"Ah," she said. "It's a multi-national business, I'm afraid. You're going to need a big net. They've got manufacturing units in China, the USA, Japan and here – in Cambridge."

Jordan didn't ask her about the third possibility of cyber warfare. He knew someone else who could tell him all about hacking into important systems. Someone with practical experience. Instead, Jordan changed the subject. "Have there been any other electrical blackouts – before Ecuador? Nothing huge or it would've been on the telly."

Raven looked at him oddly for an instant. "How do you mean?"

"If I wanted to crash a plane by turning its engines off, I'd practise on something smaller first."

"Got you." Raven thought for a moment. "I don't know. I'll trawl through a few things and let you know. But..."

"But what?"

"Bringing down a plane isn't hard. You just stop its engines and it'll crash. It'd be much harder to crash, say, a boat. Stop its engine and it just floats till someone fixes it. No one gets hurt. Just because a plane's bigger doesn't make it more difficult. Quite the opposite. To crash a boat or a car or something, you'd have to take control of its steering. That's much trickier."

"Okay," Jordan said. "Thanks."

Leaving the room, heels clicking on the shiny granite floor, Raven smiled at Kate, but she merely nodded at Jordan. There was a fleeting hint of suspicion – maybe even dislike – in her expression.

After the door closed, Kate gazed at Jordan and said, "How are you feeling about this?"

"Like I'm in Lower Stoke Boys, about to take on Manchester United."

Kate's quiet laugh was laced with nerves. "Make that both of us. But at least we've got people like Raven and Angel on our side."

The curtains slid slowly across the massive window, as if possessed by an unseen presence, cutting out daylight and the view of the Highgate tombs. Opposite the window, the giant screen unrolled itself. In seconds, the system was ready to show the CCTV footage of the ransom left in Kingston Upon Thames.

It wasn't a thriller.

In split-screen mode, there were two views of a rubbish bin taken by fixed cameras at different positions. The bin containing a black sack of money was on a tree-lined riverside path called Barge Walk. Highlights of the recording were a mum in a bright red cagoule pushing twins in a wide-load pram, an overweight jogger putting on a brave but probably unwise burst of speed, a spaniel cocking its leg against the bin, and a young black woman walking past eating a sandwich with one hand and holding a mobile to her ear with the other. Then came the significant forty-three seconds.

A slightly podgy white man entered the scene from the left. He was wearing jeans, a sweatshirt and a beanie hat. He was probably trying to look younger than he actually was. He wasn't hurrying, wasn't dawdling. He dropped a chocolate wrapper into the bin and hesitated. He looked around suspiciously and then put both hands into the bin as if he were about to lift out something heavy. He paused again. Another second or two of indecision. He straightened up, scratched his cheek and glanced round once more. Finally making up his mind, he walked away empty-handed.

"The police identified him as David Venables," Kate remarked. "A local government worker."

Jordan nodded. He had logged in to the Unit Red network and the police report was being fed directly through his optic nerve into his online brain. "They cleared him of any involvement," Jordan added. "He was going along Barge Walk, saw the black sack, decided to take a closer look and then changed his mind. 'It could have been a bomb or something,' he said when they questioned him. That's all. No interest in electronics, nothing beyond normal use of a computer, no connection to Ecuador or Edinburgh. End of the line."

"Yes," Kate replied. After a moment's thought, she added, "Or guilty but very crafty indeed."

"Not that crafty or he wouldn't have got caught on camera. And if he's Short Circuit," Jordan said, using the police's code name, "why didn't he take the money?"

"That wasn't the point, judging by the message he sent afterwards," Kate replied. "He just wanted to check he'd panicked the authorities enough to make them cough up and put millions in the bin."

Jordan sighed. "Okay. He's on a power trip. But if Short Circuit's that good, he must've known the police would put cameras in the bushes. They'd keep an eye on their cash. So, he wouldn't show up."

Kate shrugged. "Good point, but somehow he knew they'd delivered the ransom." She pressed the switch on the table and the curtains began to open. "By the way," she added, "I've got a present for you."

"Oh?"

"Angel asked me to hand it over." From behind the sofa, she produced a cardboard container, slightly bigger than a shoebox.

Inside he found a pair of shoes and a pair of gloves.

"The latest development," Kate told him. "You can't see this – not even with your eyes – but the gloves and the soles of the shoes have got tiny carbon nanotubes on them. Like the hairs on spiders' feet. Microscopic Velcro."

"So?"

"You know how Velcro sticks well, but you can ease it apart at the right angle? That means you can put the shoes and gloves on and walk up walls and across ceilings."

"Really?"

"Even surfaces that look smooth are rough under a microscope. Rough enough for flies and spiders to grip with the hairs on their feet. Rough enough for those as well," she said, pointing at his new shoes and gloves.

"Awesome."

"How do I know they'll take my weight?"

"We're putting you on a diet," she replied with a grin. "No. You'll be fine. A square metre of it holds a car up."

"Spider-Man, eh?"

"Angel said you should also know your arm's got a GPS chip in it – like a SatNav but much more precise. It's called an inertial navigation system."

"So Unit Red can spy on me?"

"It's for your own safety. We'll know where to find you if there's a problem. On top of that, you can log on with a brain implant if you get lost and it'll tell you exactly where you are. You shouldn't get lost, though, because it'll guide you wherever you want to go."

Jordan asked, "Do you listen in to what I say as well?"

Kate shook her head. "No microphones. Angel thought you wouldn't appreciate it."

"He's right."

"Back to the case," Kate said. "Where are you going to kick off?"

Jordan stopped himself from saying, "At home." After all, the Unit Red house in Highgate Cemetery was his home now. Instead, he answered, "Lower Stoke."

4 MEDWAY PIRATES

It seemed a lifetime away. In a sense, it was. A little more than a year earlier, Jordan Stryker had been ordinary Ben Smith, living in a small Medway town that had not yet been wrecked by the Thames Estuary explosion. Ben Smith had not yet been killed by the same blast. He'd got into about as much trouble as anyone else in school, he hadn't been top or bottom of his class, he'd been the brightest young tennis talent in the area, he'd played drums in a group and he'd had a best friend called Amy Goss. Among the older boys Ben knew was Merrick Breeze.

Made unrecognizable by surgery and the passage of time, Jordan walked anonymously down All Hallows Road until he came to the familiar sports centre. He didn't go inside, though. He walked straight past. On the other side, there was a wooden shed. It was large and sturdy, but still a shed. Since the Thames explosion, it had housed the local community radio station.

Before the blast, the outfit had been pirate broadcasters. Harassed by the police, the Medway Pirates had been forced to uproot themselves and move in secret from place to place. They had never been busted because Merrick Breeze had hacked into the local police computer and he'd always alerted them when a raid was about to happen. At once, volunteers had shifted the illegal gear to the next hideout. The police had found themselves scratching their heads in an empty room each time.

Merrick had also been popular with the local gangland boss, Mr. Goss – or, as Ben Smith knew him, Amy's dad. Mr. Goss had always funded the radio station and looked after Merrick in return for the opportunity to snoop on the police. Ben had never told his mum, Detective Sergeant Smith, what Merrick was doing because he'd not wanted to get a popular boy into trouble and he'd enjoyed the music that the pirates used to pump out. Anyway, it would not have been a good idea to make an enemy of Mr. Goss.

Now, as a Unit Red agent, Jordan intended to exploit his knowledge of the shared history of the radio station, Merrick and Mr. Goss. He knocked on the shed door and pushed it open with his left hand. Putting his head inside, he said, "Can I come in?"

"Yes," a big guy replied in a quiet voice. "What are you after?"

"Merrick," Jordan answered, stepping into the shed with its clutter of shelves, audio equipment, papers and CDs. In the far corner, a small area was partitioned off mostly with floor-to-ceiling windows. Through the glass, Jordan could see a DJ and a guest talking into microphones. Their interview came into the main room through speakers attached to the wall.

The producer adjusted his baseball cap and jerked his thumb towards a door on the opposite side of the shed. It looked as if it led into a broom cupboard. "Are you one of his mates?"

"Sort of. Mr. Goss sent me."

He nodded abruptly. "You'd better go in."

As always, Merrick was hunched over a computer

keypad. Jordan recognized him at once but Merrick stared back blankly.

"Hi," Jordan said, squeezing into the tiny room that could have been a broom cupboard. "I'm Jordan. Friend of Mr. Goss."

"Yeah?"

Merrick had changed. His hair was much shorter, his body more solid, his glasses more prominent, his skin more tanned, his voice deeper. He still had the broad sinewy shoulders of an Olympic swimmer but, as far as Jordan knew, he never swam. Jordan hoped something else hadn't changed. He hoped that Merrick still loved to brag about his online activities.

"I've been away," Jordan continued. "Out of touch. Last time I heard about you, you were one of the Medway Pirates."

Brought together in the confined space, Merrick was close enough to see Jordan's flaws. He glanced at the fake right arm and looked into his reconstructed face, but he didn't comment on Jordan's appearance. "Whoever decides these things thought we'd all pull together after the explosion if we had a local voice. That's us. A local community radio station. Okay, we're in a shed, but we're legal. We're broadcasting and going out over the internet. That's my bit. It's what I do instead of homework. Actually, being legit takes half the fun out of it."

Jordan smiled. "I know what you mean. You're a pretty good pirate in another way."

Merrick's face creased.

"Hacking."

"Do I know you?" Merrick asked.

"I don't think so. Just that you've got a good reputation with Mr. Goss."

Merrick nodded. "Never did like being called a hacker. Still don't. I'm a cyber joyrider."

Jordan grinned at the description. "Nice one."

Jordan had an unusual education within Unit Red. He wasn't so sure about equations and metaphors, but he'd learned a lot about the Computer Misuse Act, the Counter-Terrorism Act and intelligence work. He knew when Merrick's mischief became a crime.

"Do you hackers – I mean, cyber joyriders – mess around on your own or are you all in touch?"

Merrick wasn't entirely serious in his reply. "We're one big happy online family. Except we keep some things to ourselves. We share other things. Why?"

"Mr. Goss is wondering if you know anyone who's more cyber vandal than cyber joyrider."

"He's behind the times. There's not so much

vandalism now. It's more about making cash than making a mess. It's about identity theft and back doors to people's money." Quickly, Merrick added, "Not for me. I still like the thrill of cracking a system, not robbing people."

It was true. Jordan remembered that Merrick had never been motivated by money. He'd just enjoyed using a computer as a weapon against authority. "How about hacking into flight control systems?"

Merrick grimaced. "That's heavy."

"But do you know anyone who does it?"

"No," he answered.

"Sure?"

"Positive."

Even though Raven had told him it was easy to sabotage an aeroplane, Jordan was still wondering if Short Circuit had practised on something else first. "So, what does the happy online family take a pop at?"

Merrick laughed. "Government websites. Big business. That sort of thing. Bringing them down is fair game. And no one gets hurt."

"Any successes stick in your mind?"

"Mr. Goss knows I got into the local police computer."

"Yes, but how about other people's hits? I'm interested

– Mr. Goss is interested – in anything special."

"Special?" Merrick thought for a moment. "Well, there was one job I would've been proud of, if I'd done it. I suppose it could've been more of a cyber attack than joyriding. Anyway, it was months ago. Someone got into Cockenzie Power Station and took it offline for a day."

"Cockenzie? Where's that?"

"Edinburgh. But the hacker could have been in America or Russia or anywhere else. The net was buzzing about it for a bit. We were all trying to figure out who did it, but no one knew and no one claimed it on Zone-H…"

"Zone-H?"

"A site where joyriders log their successes. We all know *how* it was done, though."

"Oh?"

Merrick explained, "A lot of power stations, oil refineries and that sort of thing have got a really spongy software package controlling what they do. It's called SetLink. Full of holes. Whoever crashed Cockenzie sent a virus with a massive chunk of data to one of the ports running SetLink. The program couldn't cope. It shut down."

"Clever."

"Pretty simple actually. And once you know how to do it there, you can use the same tactic to get into anywhere that's running SetLink."

"How do you know who's running it?"

Merrick laughed again. "You Google 'SetLink version 1.3.1'. Then you get a list of companies."

Jordan nodded. "That *is* simple."

"Yeah. Look at it like this. A power station got hit for a day, but a cyber joyrider's done them a favour by pointing out how soft their system is. The company that makes SetLink has patched that hole now, but they'll be desperate to get their hands on the whizz-kid who did it."

"To have him arrested?"

"You've got to be joking," Merrick exclaimed. "To give him a job. They'd pay him a fortune to harden their security. And to look for faults in other companies' programs."

Jordan nodded. It made sense. Turning towards the door, he said, "I'd better let you get on now. Thanks."

Puzzled, Merrick replied, "What did Mr. Goss want? And has he got it?"

"Er...yes," Jordan muttered. "You've given him the lead he wanted."

* * *

A group of four young men had collected around Jordan's car. With his sensitive hearing, Jordan detected the voice of the one on the passenger's side. "How are we going to get in?"

They wouldn't. The Jaguar would open and start only when its computer received the right codes from Jordan's brain/computer interface – or BCI for short.

The man by the driver's door bent down and picked up half a brick. "This'll do it."

The XJ Sentinel was made of reinforced steel, Kevlar and strengthened glass. The armoured cell was bulletproof and it could withstand a grenade. Hanging back, Jordan imagined it was also brickproof.

The young man hurled the half-brick against the driver's window. It smacked against the high-tech glass, rebounded without making a mark and crashed into his shin. He yelped and clutched his leg. Jordan also flinched. He knew how painful that would be. But he also smiled.

Jordan had just talked to a cyber joyrider. These real-world joyriders were very different from Merrick Breeze. They were also far less successful. Jordan stepped forward, deciding it was time to intervene.

When they saw Jordan, the four men banded together and formed a barrier between him and the Jaguar.

"We saw it first!" one of them cried.

Jordan shook his head. "I'm not here to nick it. It's mine."

"You're not old enough – or posh enough."

"If you just walk away, that'll be the end of it," he said. "I won't report you."

"No chance!" The man with the bruised shin limped towards him threateningly.

Jordan stood his ground and scanned them with his terahertz vision. They weren't carrying any obvious weapons.

"Why should we leave you to it?"

"Because it's mine," Jordan replied.

The man laughed and then, trying to catch Jordan off guard, suddenly aimed a punch at his head.

Amazingly fast, Jordan's right hand came up in front of his face and the man's fist slammed into it. He cried out again, partly in shock this time, and nursed his bruised knuckles.

"Not your lucky day, is it?" said Jordan. "Best give up."

Another one stepped forward. "Why? You're outnumbered."

"If I thump you, I might take your head off completely. On top of that, the car's going to start in five seconds and, if you don't get out of the way, it'll mow you down."

They all sniggered.

Jordan hadn't practised the remote manoeuvre but his BCI was capable of operating the Jaguar from a short distance. He transmitted the first code.

The men looked round as the car came to life with a slight growl. Unsure, they glanced at one another.

When Jordan sent the code to reverse, the car began to move towards the group.

Panicking, they ran off.

With a grin on his face, Jordan stopped the car, unlocked it with a thought and got in.

5 BEFORE ECUADOR

Raven looked up from her monitor and said, "I've been scouring databases, the internet and every news outlet I can think of, looking for unexplained downtime or known cyber attacks before the Ecuador spectacular. I've been ringing round as well, but most organizations won't admit anything's got through their defences. It'd be like advertising a weakness, so they keep quiet. Private companies are the worst. They want everyone to think their security is foolproof."

"But you've got something, right?" Jordan replied.

"A few things. There was one very public breakdown. The National Lottery computer died a death on live TV in January. It could have been a glitch. It could have been Short Circuit, I suppose. The Commission won't talk about it. That'd tell other geeks it's fun to target high-profile computers."

"As if they didn't know," Jordan muttered.

"Norton – the anti-virus people – had an unexplained evening offline. So did Amazon." Raven scanned the notes on her screen. "Here's a horrible one. A woman in Felixstowe Hospital died when she was undergoing brain surgery. A robotic arm was destroying cancer tissue when it suffered a mysterious fault. It doesn't bear thinking about. The laser fired off in all directions instead of keeping to the tumour."

Jordan asked, "Who was she?"

"A woman called..." Raven glanced down at her monitor again. "Paige Ottaway. Married, mum of three. There was an inquest. One of the motherboards in the robot packed up so it was put down to equipment failure, but it could have been a cyber attack."

"Anything else?"

"Someone hacked into NatWest's central computer and disabled it for hours. The bankers lost a day's pay. That's an annual salary to you and me. Trinity College Dublin and a Scottish power station got stung as well. A few councils have been attacked. And those are just the ones I found in Britain and Ireland. There'll be quite a few more keeping quiet, ones I didn't spot, and plenty overseas."

"What about us?"

"Us? Unit Red?"

Jordan nodded. "Yes."

"Never had a problem. No incursions at all."

"Would you admit it if we had?"

"Within Unit Red, yes. No one outside knows about us anyway, so they wouldn't ask. Or target us in the first place."

"Okay," Jordan said. "Did you try Zone-H?"

"Yes. It's where hackers show off about defacing other people's sites. There's probably a good dose of exaggeration in there. It lists thousands of attacks. Too many really, but nothing jumped out at me. All it did was confirm the strikes on the National Lottery, Norton, quite a few councils and the NatWest Bank were malicious. I've put everything in a file for you, but..."

"What?"

Raven shrugged. "They might not have anything to do with Short Circuit. Some'll be kids flexing their virtual muscles."

"I know." Jordan sighed and then added, "Can you try something? It might be daft, but... There was the crash in Edinburgh and, before that, the plane from Quito to Amsterdam. Short Circuit asked for the money in Kingston and he sends his sound files to Manchester. Can you do an internet search on Quito, Amsterdam, Edinburgh, Kingston and Manchester? I'm wondering if there's a connection, but I don't know why there should be."

"All right," Raven replied.

In a third of a second, the search engine came up with an answer. None of its finds contained a reference to all five places. The first page of results was mostly about flights and tourism.

"Let's add Felixstowe and Dublin," Jordan suggested. "Where the woman died and the university got hit. Just in case."

It didn't help. The new search revealed more links to shipping information.

Angel strode into the room, looking as if he had something important to say, but instead he was captivated by their computer research.

"One more thing," said Jordan. "Try Ecuador instead of Quito."

This time, the top two results were both links to sites

featuring the lyrics of a song by a group called Lemon Jelly. Raven clicked on the first hit and the words of "Ramblin' Man" filled the screen. "Not so much lyrics," she said, "as a list of places."

Excited, Jordan pointed to each place name in turn. "Look. Kingston, Felixstowe, Ecuador, Edinburgh, Amsterdam, Manchester and Dublin. They're all there."

"It's a long list," Raven noted. "That means it could be a coincidence. The bigger the list, the more likely all Short Circuit's significant places will be on it."

Behind them, Angel butted in. "Sudbury, by any chance?"

Jordan scanned the lyrics and then looked at Angel. "Yes, it's there!"

Angel nodded. "A new warning's just come in," he explained. "Something's going to happen there tomorrow. That's why I came to see you."

"What sort of something?"

"Short Circuit didn't say, but I want you in Sudbury."

"Where is it?"

"There are a few, but he talked about the Suffolk version. I've arranged for you to spend the day with the emergency services. Kate will go with you. She'll blend in because of her background."

Before Angel recruited her into Unit Red, Kate had

been a firefighter. On duty at the time of the Thames Estuary explosion, she had found the severely injured Ben Smith in the ruins of his home. She had refused to give up on him. She had saved his life.

"But what do we do?" Jordan asked Angel.

"Keep your eyes open and wait for something to happen."

Victoria Truman's high-tech home was an oddity among the bright pink Suffolk cottages. At its heart was a computer that monitored and controlled almost every aspect of living within the modern house. Modified to allow her to live independently now that her health had worsened, the building was stuffed with sensors. They controlled the temperature, humidity, hot water and light level. They alerted Victoria when she left the bath water running, the oven on, or a pan on the hob. They alerted a care company if she fell over and didn't get up again. When she left the house, the sensors transmitted a message to her mobile phone to tell her if she'd left a door or a window open.

Two years previously, she'd been a lively, talkative and popular sixty-year-old. She'd been a regular at dancing, swimming and hiking. Then her occasional absences became more than occasional. She'd simply forget to go to the old folks' activities or she'd lack the energy, preferring to slump in her armchair. Increasingly, she became more absent-minded and less mobile. Worse, she didn't seem concerned that she was missing out on the things she used to enjoy. It was as if she'd forgotten that she'd once had fun.

Despite looking at friends as if she'd never seen them before, despite losing her enthusiasm for life, the neighbours still called, made cups of tea and talked to her. No one was mean to her, no one egged her house or called her names. Until someone did something much worse. Someone crashed her computer. Someone stopped the sensors alerting her to the fact that she'd not turned off the gas. Or maybe someone even had enough control over her computer to make it turn *on* the gas.

On the way to Sudbury, Jordan and Kate listened to the version of "Ramblin' Man" that Jordan had downloaded onto his car's computer. Cleverly superimposed on a dance tune, a man's sampled voice recited all of the places he had visited. But there was no obvious reason why Short Circuit might hijack the lyrics for a killing spree.

When they reached the Suffolk town, they could have

hung out with the police, the ambulance staff or the fire service. In the event of a disaster, all three would receive an emergency call at the same time. Jordan and Kate could be on the scene in the first wave. Angel had cleared the way for them to visit the fire station. It was obvious to Jordan that Kate relished looking round the place and chatting to the firefighters. He guessed that, for her, it brought back fond memories. For Jordan, the waiting was dull.

No aeroplanes fell from the sky and landed on sleepy Sudbury. No bombs went off. There wasn't even a power cut. There was a hoax call in the morning and a traffic accident in the afternoon. The fire officers had to cut an injured driver out of his car. It was nearly evening when a 999 call reported a house on fire.

"Is this it?" Kate asked. "A house going up in flames?"

Jordan shrugged. "Not exactly the end of civilization."

The officer on the phone shouted over her shoulder, "Neighbour says it's an old disabled woman living on her own in a computer-controlled house."

At once, Jordan and Kate looked at each other and nodded. A home with that sort of technology could be a target for Short Circuit.

They hitched a ride to the emergency. When they got there, broken glass was falling from the windows of the house and flames were flashing from the holes. In Jordan's sensitive ears, the fire roared. Horrified neighbours were standing around with their hands over their mouths. By the time the firefighters directed their hoses at the blazing house, the door and window frames had blackened completely. The right-hand side of the roof had caved in and tiles were collapsing into the hole.

Jordan turned away. The temperature was so high that the whole place glowed intense yellow in the infrared part of his vision. The brightness was too much for him.

A sudden explosion made him turn back. The solar panel on the left-hand side of the roof had shattered and a large glass tube was hurtling like a javelin towards one of the firefighters. Its edge was a circle of jagged glass. The fireman had frozen, terrified. The tube would not just pierce him. Like a rapidly moving bullet, it would go straight through him. A neighbour screamed as Jordan launched himself in front of the officer. His artificial arm intercepted the deadly arrow, clipping its side and deflecting it from its course.

Jordan hit the ground and rolled over twice before he could look back. The glass javelin was poking out of a flower bed and the firefighter was blinking, recovering from the near miss. He looked down at Jordan and said, "Are you okay?"

Jordan got to his feet. "No problem. Are you?"

The officer took a deep breath and nodded. "Yes. Thanks. I've...er..."

"Got a job to do?"

"Yes." Before he made for one of the fire appliances, he said, "Thanks again."

Once the hoses had done their job and the heat was bearable, a firefighter in full protective gear went inside, but he was too late to save the life of the only occupant. Victoria Truman had succumbed to toxic fumes well before the fire had reached her body.

What else could Jordan do? At the scene, there were only shocked friends and neighbours. There was no sign of a bad guy running away. If Short Circuit had hacked into her computer, he could have been on the far side of the planet but, according to Raven, if he'd used an e-bomb or hardware Trojan, he'd have needed to be quite close. Then, if the fire really was his handiwork, he would probably have left the area well before the emergency services arrived. There was no one to chase, nothing requiring the power of a bionic agent.

Jordan and Kate talked to some of Victoria's neighbours, gathering information about her, but they heard nothing that helped them to understand why Short Circuit might attack her. They hung around in Sudbury until late, yet there was no spectacular show of strength. If Short Circuit had struck, he'd destroyed one house and one elderly life.

To Jordan, it seemed pathetic and pointless. But he remembered Short Circuit's message. He could almost hear the voice announcing that he was going to target some individuals before he targeted everyone.

Jordan also had his mum's words of wisdom in his head. "People who fail don't plan to fail, they just fail to plan." What was Jordan's plan for catching Short Circuit? He didn't really have one. He knew only that he needed more links between Short Circuit's attacks. The big attacks and the small ones. There had to be a reason for both.

Using his wireless connection to the Unit Red computer, he checked the police records again. The investigating team had put all of the names of the victims from the Quito tragedy alongside the list of everyone onboard Flight LH6681 from Edinburgh to Heathrow and cross-checked the two files. There were no obvious links, like family or business partners. There were bankers, nurses, teachers and power company workers on both flights. One person on each flight worked for

Apple. Thirteen people on the flight from Ecuador and thirty-seven passengers boarding at Edinburgh lived in London. All of these possible connections had been investigated and considered insignificant.

But now, Jordan had more names. Short Circuit had warned them that he'd strike in Sudbury, so Victoria Truman was almost certainly one of his victims. Paige Ottaway from Felixstowe could have been another.

Driving back to London, he contacted Raven on the car's secure hands-free phone. "I think you should add Victoria Truman to the mix," he said. "Does the computer come up with anything now?"

"Okay," Raven said slowly, as she entered instructions at her terminal. "Hang on. It's trying... No. There's nothing obvious. It'll need more time to look for anything more subtle. I'll let you know."

Jordan overtook a lorry with an easy burst of speed. "Why don't we throw Paige Ottaway in as well?"

Raven's voice was clear above the low drone of the engine. "I know Felixstowe's in that song, but it's not certain she's got anything to do with Short Circuit."

"Just try it and see, maybe."

Raven hesitated but, after a split second, she agreed. "All right. If that's what you want. I'll get back to you if it turns anything up."

"Thanks."

Twenty minutes later, just as Jordan and Kate were going under the M25, Raven returned his call. This time, there was tension in her voice. "The computer's finished churning through the data," she said, "and it could be onto something."

6 POWER FAILURE

Jordan and Kate returned well after midnight. Even so, Angel called the team together in the bunker. He looked first at Raven. "Okay. Tell us what you've got."

"We know Victoria Truman's from Sudbury in Suffolk. Lived there all her life. Phil Lazenby – captain of the Edinburgh flight – lives in Long Melford, on the rare occasions he's at home. That's just up the road from Sudbury. He was born and brought up round the corner in Ipswich. One passenger on the Quito flight came from

Woodbridge in the same area. His name was Carlton Reed."

"Carlton Reed," Jordan muttered to himself.

"What is it?" Angel asked.

"I thought I recognized..." Jordan shrugged. "No. It doesn't matter."

Raven finished by saying, "And there's Paige Ottaway – the one who died in hospital at the end of January. She lived just outside Felixstowe, Suffolk."

"We can't put her down as a certain Short Circuit casualty, can we?" Angel replied.

"No," Raven admitted.

"But there's still a Suffolk connection," Jordan said.

Angel nodded slowly. He wasn't agreeing. He was thinking. "It would mean we're prepared to believe Short Circuit brought down an entire plane to kill one man from Suffolk: Carlton Reed. We'd also have to believe he tried to repeat the performance to murder Captain Lazenby." He analysed their faces, one after the other. "Like me, you're finding that hard to swallow, Kate."

"Yes."

"Raven isn't sure and you, Jordan, think there's something in it."

At the same time, Jordan and Raven both said, "Yes."

"So, we have a difference of opinion. But it's *possible* Suffolk's just a coincidence. Yes?"

Jordan sighed. "I suppose."

"By the same token, it's possible it isn't," Angel continued. "So we need to look into it. Since you believe in it most, Jordan, you check it out."

"Okay. But..."

Angel smiled, anticipating his question. "You should consider yourself lucky that Short Circuit didn't manage to destroy the Edinburgh plane and its pilot. You have a witness. It'd be interesting if Captain Lazenby knew Victoria Truman, Carlton Reed and Paige Ottaway when they were alive, wouldn't it? If he did, you'd convince us all that Suffolk's the common denominator."

Jordan nodded eagerly. "I'll go and find out." He hesitated before adding, "I'll get photos of them – in case he only knew them by sight."

Using the laptop on Angel's desk, Raven soon located Captain Lazenby. "He's just landed in Stockholm, Sweden," she reported, "but after an overnight rest, he's flying into Heathrow. He's got to be here tomorrow." She looked up at Jordan and said, "What's up? You look...."

"Stockholm's one of the places in that song."

"You think he's in danger?" Kate asked.

Jordan nodded.

"I disagree," Angel said. "Short Circuit won't attack another plane piloted by Lazenby. If he did, we'd know for sure who he's after. That'd be revealing too much about himself."

"Does he care?"

Angel thought for an instant. "He enjoys being mysterious. He enjoys the fact that we don't know where he is and why he's doing what he's doing. He likes us to know only what he tells us in his messages."

Jordan shrugged.

"What could we do anyway?" said Kate. "Tell Lazenby to be careful, or not to fly back?"

Raven stifled a yawn. "He's booked to be in Ipswich Town Hall tomorrow night."

"Why?" Jordan asked.

"Apparently, his home town's giving him an award for bravery. He's already been given the Freedom of the City of Edinburgh. He's become something of a celebrity since the crash, but a reluctant one. He's never talked about it. Not in public. Tomorrow, it's a private ceremony. No cameras, no press. Just a council photographer to snap the occasion."

"Was Ipswich in the 'Ramblin' Man' lyrics?" Kate asked.

"Ipanema, yes, but not Ipswich," Raven replied with

a grin. "Brazil or Suffolk. I know where I'd rather be."

"*You* don't have a choice, Jordan," said Angel. "Make your way over to Ipswich tomorrow. I'll get you a pass into the award ceremony. And I'll tell a contact in the local police what's happening. They can prime Lazenby so he's expecting to talk to you."

Jordan felt relieved. His fears about the Stockholm flight had come to nothing. There hadn't been another aeroplane disaster so he could speak to Phil Lazenby after the pilot had received the Freedom of the Borough of Ipswich. The task was important but easy.

The paved square outside the gothic building was alive with people. Some gathered in small groups, some strode past on their way to somewhere else, some went up the steps and through the Town Hall's imposing arches below the clock tower.

A steward eyed Jordan suspiciously and checked his pass carefully before welcoming him into the Town Hall. "Good evening, Sir. Can I remind you that we're not allowing cameras or phones that take pictures tonight? You can leave any such devices with the cloakroom staff. Then you can go right in and take your seat." He waved his arm towards the ground-floor chamber.

Jordan nodded, but he had no intention of handing over his mobile. He might need it in an emergency. He asked, "Has Captain Lazenby arrived?"

"I believe so, Sir. I imagine he's being treated to a glass of champagne."

"Thanks."

Jordan cringed. He didn't like being called *sir*. The whole occasion was far too formal for his tastes. Looking round at the other male guests, he realized that he was the only one without a suit and tie. He stood out in his black trousers, black sweatshirt and leather jacket. When people turned and glanced disapprovingly at him, he told himself that they were merely guests of the council while he was on an important mission. He also smiled internally at the thought that he owned the most expensive car parked in the area.

Jordan went straight into the windowless chamber because he thought people would not stare so much if he made himself less visible by sitting down. At the front of the room was a raised row of ornate wooden seats for about eight people. That's where the Lord Mayor and Phil Lazenby would sit, no doubt. Facing them were several rows of semicircular benches for the guests. Jordan took a seat at the end of the first row.

When everyone had assembled, a door on Jordan's

side of the chamber opened. The room hushed as the dignitaries filed in and glided towards the thrones at the front. When they'd settled, the mayor leaned towards the microphone and said, "Welcome to the Town Hall on this auspicious occasion as we celebrate an outstanding achievement by one of our own sons. I am delighted..."

Reminded of his old school's speech day, Jordan took a deep breath. It was going to be a long dull evening, full of never-ending lectures. He turned down his hearing, studied the weird wooden carvings in front of the panel of speakers and then focused on Captain Lazenby. The fifty-year-old was dressed in a neat pilot's uniform, but, outside of an aeroplane's cockpit, he looked out of place and embarrassed. He wore a fixed grin. It was probably an attempt to hide his discomfort.

The Leader of the Council talked at length about pride in Ipswich and its people. Then someone else went through the events of Monday 5th March. Behind the speaker, on the bland wall, was projected the news coverage of Captain Lazenby's amazing life-saving splash-down in the Firth of Forth.

Without warning, the film flickered and died. At the same time, the announcer's amplified voice was replaced by her natural quiet tone and all of the lights went out.

There were gasps of surprise, shock and annoyance.

From the front, an authoritative voice boomed. "Ladies and gentlemen. It seems we have a power cut. Please remain calm. Stay exactly where you are – we're all perfectly safe as long as we don't start stumbling around – until the stewards can provide emergency lighting or someone replaces the fuse. I'm sure it'll only be a moment."

Jordan was having none of it. Immediately tense, he guessed that the failure of the electricity supply was the work of Short Circuit. He imagined that Phil Lazenby was in imminent danger. Ignoring the announcement, he decided to act without hesitation. The room might be a blackout to everyone else, but not to him. Switching to infrared vision, all of the nearby people were recognizable. Further away, they were yellowy blobs. The chamber was various shades of rippling grey.

No one was making for Phil Lazenby. No one was threatening him. Yet.

Jordan strode to the front and mounted the steps.

Hearing the footfalls, the council leader said, "Please remain seated, everyone. It won't be long."

A joker among the visitors called out, "Cut off, eh? You'd think the council would pay its energy bills."

"Or find a torch," someone else added.

Fearing that Short Circuit could make his next move

at any instant, Jordan sneaked up to Captain Lazenby and touched his shoulder.

In the darkness, the pilot stiffened but he didn't jump in shock. He was practised at keeping his composure.

Jordan whispered directly into his ear. "I'm Jordan Stryker. Someone's told you about me, haven't they? I'm here to protect you." His words were lost to everyone else in the murmur and occasional giggle coming from the bemused audience.

Phil turned towards Jordan and nodded. "Yes. But how do I know you're..."

Jordan was scanning the rest of the hall. Someone else was sneaking towards the front. It was a big man and he was stumbling around in the blackness. His right arm was stretched out in front of him, as if holding something, but Jordan couldn't make out what it was. The object was cold. It didn't have an infrared signal.

Quickly, Jordan extracted his ID and phone. He used the faint glow from his mobile to illuminate his identity card.

"Okay."

"Grab my arm," Jordan whispered. "I've got to get you out of here right now."

One of the officials called, "I'm sorry about this. Are you all right, Captain Lazenby?"

"Yes," he called out.

"Someone's coming this way," Jordan said quietly to the pilot. "It's too risky here. Follow me before..."

There was a thump as the approaching man accidently kicked the end of one of the benches.

Phil's reply was also hushed. "All right."

Jordan led him to the end of the raised platform.

"Captain Lazenby?" the mayor called out.

He said, "I'm just... It's okay. No worries."

"Steps down here," Jordan whispered. But when he looked up, he realized he wasn't going to get Phil Lazenby to the side door before the man closed in on them.

Jordan could make out his features now. He was tall and broad-shouldered, with very short hair and prominent ears. He was wearing a suit and tie. In his extended right hand was a gun.

Phil Lazenby came down the steps slowly and unsteadily, feeling each one first with his foot.

When he reached the bottom, Jordan didn't say anything. He didn't want to give the gunman any clues on the pilot's position. Jordan simply grabbed Phil's arm and urgently tugged him towards the door.

But the guy with the gun would crash into them before they reached it.

Jordan stepped forward, raised his artificial arm and brought it down somewhere between the man's right elbow and wrist. There was a piercing cry of pain and a clatter as the weapon hit the floor.

Jordan kicked the gun away, then thrust the door open and dragged the Captain through it as quickly as he could. Behind him, the chamber erupted with quizzical cries. In the next room, Jordan slammed the door shut and looked around. His night vision picked out a heavy table. He dragged it across the doorway to delay anyone who tried to follow them.

"Come on," Jordan said. "We're not safe yet. If he finds his gun..."

"Gun?" Phil spluttered.

"Yes. He was aiming a gun at you."

"But... How do you know? How are you...?"

Jordan didn't want to explain about his capabilities. "Always been good at seeing in the dark. Come on. I'll guide you again. There's a door over there. It'll be a way out."

"Yes," the pilot agreed. "It's where we came in. It goes into a corridor that leads back to the entrance."

"Good. We've got to get out."

"But what's going on?"

"I'll tell you – in a minute." He tugged Captain Lazenby's arm. "This way."

The foyer was in chaos. There was enough light coming from the lamps in the square to stop officials bumping into each other, the furniture and the pillars, but not enough of a glow to see exactly what was going on. Jordan and the pilot slipped out unnoticed.

"Round the back," Jordan said, breaking into a jog. "You'll be okay in my car."

Reluctantly, the pilot followed at a trot.

When Jordan came to a halt and the Jaguar door clicked open, Captain Lazenby let out a short gasp. "This is yours?"

Jordan nodded. "Get in. I'll lock it from out here so you're safe."

Halfway inside, Phil asked, "What are you going to do?"

"I've got to go back."

"Why?"

"To get the man with the gun," Jordan replied. "Before I go, do you know Victoria Truman, Carlton Reed or Paige Ottaway?"

Phil thought for a moment and then shook his head. "I don't think so. Sorry. Doesn't ring any bells."

"Try their pictures, then." Jordan took them out of the inner pocket of his jacket.

Reaching for the photographs, Captain Lazenby

looked doubtful. "I come across a lot of people in my line of work, but I'll see if I can put my finger on anything."

"Thanks. Turn the light on – it's just above your head – and take a look while I'm inside."

"Will do."

Jordan shut the door, locked it with his BCI and steeled himself for his next ordeal.

7 ARMED RESPONSE

Running round to the front of the darkened building, Jordan didn't hesitate for long on the steps outside. He stood a better chance against Short Circuit – if that's who was inside – before the lamps came back on. His engineered eyes gave him an advantage in the dark, even if Short Circuit had been able to fumble around on the floor and find his gun.

Jordan sped past the stewards. Two of them had located torches and beams of light were flashing from side to side like unruly headlights. Jordan didn't believe for a moment that they'd keep the torches to themselves and leave the audience in total darkness. By now, the crowded chamber must have emergency lamps. He had no choice but to confront the gunman in the light.

Then it happened. Like a firework illuminating the night sky, the lighting suddenly flared and the whole building shone brightly. Jordan's delicate cameras took an instant to adjust and his hearing picked up the ironic cheers from the council chamber.

He took a breath and then made for the hall. Just as he was reaching out for the handle, the door opened and the broad-shouldered man was standing in his way. He was holding his right arm gingerly against his stomach.

Unsure, Jordan hesitated.

In that moment, the gunman reached into his inner pocket awkwardly with his left hand.

Jordan prepared his robotic arm.

"Plain-clothes officer, Suffolk Police," the man said. Wincing, he produced his badge and showed it to Jordan. "Armed Response Unit." Then he demanded, "Stay still. Keep your hands well out where I can see them."

Jordan let out a breath. "I'm Jordan Stryker..."

"Show me your ID. Don't try anything."

Slowly, Jordan took the card from his pocket, making

sure the officer could see that he was extracting a bit of plastic and not a weapon. He held it out.

The policeman looked at it and nodded. "Let me see your right hand. I was told it's false."

Jordan held it out and clenched his fist. The motors in each finger made a muted hum.

At last, the police officer relaxed. "I don't know what you do, but we were notified you'd be here." He smiled wryly and added, "I can't say it's been a pleasure to meet you..."

"Sorry about your arm. I thought you were... Anyway, have I broken it?"

"I heard a crack. I imagine the bone's fractured."

"Does it hurt?"

"Like hell."

"Sorry," Jordan repeated. "I was protecting..."

He nodded. "I know. I'd have done the same. I should've given a spoken warning in there, but I didn't want to panic anyone. That would've made everything much worse. I couldn't see anything, but I heard someone – you – creeping around at the front. That was worrying because the man who told us about you mentioned a potential threat to Captain Lazenby. That's why I'm on duty."

"You looked pretty threatening to me."

The policeman said, "No hard feelings. But there's something more important."

"Oh?"

"What have you done with the guest-of-honour?"

"Ah. Yes. I'll go and get him. He's safe. In my car. But...er...what about the power cut?"

The police officer smiled again. "They found a smoking rat in the basement, apparently. It bit through the mains supply. Nothing to do with terrorism." He gave Jordan's shoulder a friendly slap. "You give them their local hero and I'll get myself an ambulance."

Jordan hesitated. "It's already on its way."

"Is it?"

"I can hear it – just."

"I can't," the officer said. "Who called for it? Not me."

Jordan frowned. A shiver ran the length of his body. He had a horrible feeling that something might have happened to Phil Lazenby. He took off again. The policeman followed him as quickly as the throbbing in his arm allowed.

Jordan skidded to a halt on King Street where he'd had special permission to leave the XJ. But there was nothing. It had gone. His breath came in short gasps as the full horror of the situation struck him.

Clutching his injured arm, the officer slowed to a stop. "I can hear the siren now. It's getting closer." He pointed towards the Butter Market. "Looks like something's going off down the road."

On the corner, there was a small cluster of people around the entrance to a shop – a shop that must be closed at this time in the evening.

They both broke into a run again.

As they approached, Jordan could see that the people were standing around his car. Plainly, the Jag had accelerated along the street, mounted the pavement and rammed the concrete arch of the shopfront.

The officer shouted, "Police!" and showed his ID card as he pushed his way through the bunch of people. "Get back, please."

"We can't open it," someone yelled. "He's locked in."

"I've called an ambulance."

When Jordan saw what had happened to Captain Lazenby, he turned aside, unable to concentrate on the code for unlocking the car door.

Behind him, a man muttered, "It must be built like a tank. Hardly a scratch but... No seat belt. He's all over the windscreen."

"It's awful," said the woman standing next to him. "Poor man."

"I wonder who he is. He's in a uniform of some sort."

The policeman spread out his left arm and pleaded with the nosy onlookers. "Back off. Give him a bit of privacy, please. And leave room for the ambulance."

The sightseers shuffled away, but only by a few metres. They seemed to be transfixed by the tragedy.

Jordan forced himself to look back into the car. It was clear that, when the car had come to a sudden stop, Phil's body had kept going. The airbag hadn't activated. The passenger hadn't stood a chance.

Finally, Jordan summoned the strength and concentration to transmit the code and the doors unlocked. He couldn't hear the quiet click because an ambulance was screaming up Prince's Street. It stopped in the middle of the road.

When the crew turned off the siren, the town seemed morbidly quiet. Two paramedics rushed to the side of Jordan's car. Leaning in from opposite sides, they reached the same conclusion at once. They went through the usual tests, but they already knew the outcome. When they stood up straight, they both shook their heads.

The officer showed them his badge. "You can't do anything for him?"

"Sorry."

The policeman let out a long weary breath. "Don't move him. It's probably a crime scene. But you can do something for me. I need someone to fix my arm. It's fractured, I think. First..." Seeing a patrol car drawing up, he added, "Let me brief the uniformed guys and call for reinforcements." He turned to Jordan and asked, "Are you okay?"

Jordan took his phone and said, "I've got an emergency number. I guess it's time to use it."

The officer nodded sympathetically. "You do that. I'll get rid of the crowd. And send someone to the Town Hall when we've got enough people to deal with this."

Jordan stared into the car where three crumpled photographs lay on the bloodied seat beside the pilot's body. He would never know if Phil Lazenby had recognized the faces.

It was Angel who answered the Unit Red crisis number. Jordan tried to give his boss a clear account of what had occurred, but it wasn't easy when his brain was blunted by numbness.

"All right, Jordan," Angel said. "I sort of get the picture. Kate's gone home and I don't know where Raven is, but she's not here. I'll get myself helicoptered over to you. Won't be long."

* * *

It was late. Very late. Jordan and Angel were the only customers in an all-night café. Force-feeding Jordan strong coffee, Angel stressed, "It wasn't your fault. It wasn't as if you left the handbrake off on a hill. You just provided the car. Someone else was driving – remotely – and crashed it deliberately. It's called sudden unintended acceleration. I think we know who's got the right bag of tricks to take control of the on-board computer. He used your car as a murder weapon."

"But I left the captain there. If I hadn't locked the doors..."

Angel interrupted. "You put him in what you thought was the most secure place."

"I bet another agent..."

"Would have done the same."

"But..."

"Everything's easy with hindsight. You did a good job with the information you had at the time." Angel lowered his voice in the empty café. "Anyway, I can't criticize. I said Short Circuit wouldn't attack Lazenby again because that'd tell us too much about him."

Jordan liked to think the head of Unit Red was infallible but, right now, he felt strangely comforted to know that even Angel could make a mistake.

"He was here, wasn't he?" said Jordan. "Short Circuit, I mean."

Angel nodded. "Planes take off from predictable places at predictable times. Even if they're delayed, he can find out when to attack by looking at a departure board live on the internet. He might not have to be anywhere near. Tonight was different. Lazenby getting into your car wasn't predictable. Short Circuit would've had to be here in Ipswich to know. I don't suppose you saw anyone loitering around where you parked?"

"No."

"He must have thought it was his lucky day," Angel whispered. "No doubt, he came to see – or stop – Lazenby getting his award, found the Town Hall in complete darkness and spotted his victim sitting in a car full of microchips. A gift." He spread his arms in a gesture of helplessness. "You weren't to know. It's a worrying development, though."

"How do you mean?"

"He didn't just knock out electrical components this time. Far more sophisticated than what he did with the planes. He got enough control over the circuits to start the Jag and accelerate. That's electromagnetic interference with the electronic throttle, I imagine. He wouldn't need anything else, like steering or braking."

"Does that mean he could...?" Jordan pointed to the side of his head.

"No. He couldn't make you do things you don't want to do. He might be able to take over your brain implants, but they don't control you, so he can't either. They just help you to live. You're a human being. You have free will."

Jordan sighed and sipped more coffee.

"According to the local force," Angel added, "one witness was a driving instructor, so we can probably trust his judgement. He said the car was doing about eighty kilometres an hour and still speeding up when it hit the wall. That means Short Circuit disabled the airbag as well. He wouldn't have hung around after that. He would've slipped away."

Jordan asked, "What happens now?"

"I supply a story to the press. No mention of you and your car. A gagging order will take care of any witnesses who say something different." He took a moment to think. "Lazenby had a bit too much champagne at the reception and had to leave. Maybe he was called away unexpectedly to some emergency. He jumped into his car and drove on too much alcohol. No one else involved."

"Can't you do it without blaming him?"

"I know it's a pity to sully a hero, but... No choice, I'm afraid." Angel finished his coffee. "A lorry's coming over to take the Jag back. I'll put every engineer we've got on it. New chips from a different source – so they can't have Trojans in them. Bigger, better security – harder to hack. Then we need a way forward. You can put all this behind you by cracking on with the case."

"I suppose."

"Any ideas?"

"I'm not really in the mood."

Angel nodded. "You have proved a link, you know. You were right. Picking on Phil Lazenby twice can't be a coincidence. It looks like Short Circuit's after specific people in Suffolk, even if we don't know why."

"Or who's next," Jordan replied.

"Come on," Angel said, getting to his feet. "There's a chopper waiting for us."

8 TIP-OFF

Jordan couldn't sleep. His brain replayed the evening's events over and over again. He tried to clear his mind, or think about something else, but, before long, he was talking once more to Phil Lazenby in Ipswich and deciding to leave him in the Jaguar before returning to the Town Hall. The playback skipped. He was staring at the smeared stain on the windscreen and the body that had been thrown forward at high speed before slumping back onto the seat and falling sideways.

Jordan was damp with sweat and he felt queasy. Some unseen torturer seemed to have placed a belt around his stomach and was pulling it tighter and tighter. Another imaginary band was squeezing his skull.

Just as his bedroom curtain began to glow with morning sunshine, Jordan finally drifted into uneasy sleep. His internal clock woke him long before his body had refreshed itself. He felt groggy and grumpy as he dressed. He had no choice but to get up, though. It was Sunday and he was due to meet Angel and Raven in the bunker.

They'd hardly begun to talk when Kate Stelfox called from the workshop above them. "I think you'd better come up," she said. "There's something you should see."

The three of them darted to the lift, went up to ground level and rushed into the garage.

Jordan noticed straight away that the engineers had cleaned the inside of his car thoroughly. The awful stains had vanished completely. Anyone examining the Jaguar would not find a trace of what had happened to the passenger.

One engineer was delving under the bonnet, like a pathologist examining a dead body. An IT specialist was conducting a post-mortem on the car's computer and black-box recorder.

Kate was holding three pieces of creased and tainted

paper. "The photos you gave him, Jordan. Did you write anything on the back?"

"No."

"Check out Paige Ottaway's picture."

Jordan took it in his artificial hand and avoided touching the brown bloodstain. He turned the photograph over while Angel and Raven, standing either side of him, watched eagerly. He caught his breath when he realized that Phil Lazenby had jotted something on the reverse. He had written in clear block capitals: *FOREW*.

"Forew? Why did he do that? What does it mean?"

"Maybe it's an acronym," Angel said. "We'll find out back in the bunker."

"Is it a word?" Jordan asked.

"Not that I'm aware of," Angel replied. "It might not be complete. Perhaps he was interrupted when the car took off. Apparently, he had a pen in his hand when he died."

Kate said, "Was he dyslexic or anything? Maybe terrible at spelling?"

"A pilot? Probably not. But we need to make sure." Angel turned towards the door. "Come on. We're going to look into the history of all four victims. That includes Phil Lazenby's writing skills." Over his shoulder, he said, "Thanks, Kate. Carry on with the car."

* * *

Back in the bunker, Raven soon completed a search. Scanning down the list of results, she said, "Forew's a surname but it's very uncommon. Mostly, the internet thinks it's short for foreword. That's all. It's not a known acronym. Hang on. I'll double-check in a dictionary." Her fingers flew across the keypad again. "No," she added a few moments later. "Nothing."

"Okay," Angel replied. "We're not getting anywhere with it right now. We need a change of direction."

"The Lemon Jelly song?" Raven suggested.

Angel groaned. "Now Short Circuit's struck in Ipswich – not in the lyrics – the song's probably irrelevant. A red herring. Let's get to the point. There's got to be something common to Phil Lazenby, Victoria Truman, Carlton Reed and maybe Paige Ottaway as well."

Trying to lighten the mood, Raven said, "Yes. He can't just be killing the people of Suffolk for painting their houses that horrible pink colour."

"He's not doing it with an e-bomb either," Angel said.

Raven nodded. "An electronic bomb would cripple Jordan's car, not make it go. We're down to hacking or a hardware Trojan. Although..."

"What?"

"If it was a Trojan, it was an advanced one that allows you to take control of a circuit board, not just kill it. I don't know how, but rumour has it that they exist."

Jordan shook his head. "I'm still trying to get used to the idea that it's easier to down a great big plane than crash a car into a wall."

"It's not the size of the target that's important," Raven explained. "It's the complexity of the electronic attack."

"I guess so." Surprising the other two, Jordan asked, "Is there a program called SetLink in my car?"

Angel didn't know. He turned to Raven.

"SetLink?" she said. "Yes. It's the industry standard for controlling systems, especially power."

"Who makes it?"

"Why?"

"Because it's been targeted by a hacker before. That's how the power station in Edinburgh copped it."

"How do you know?" Angel asked.

"I spoke to a cyber joyrider."

He laughed. "Is that what they call themselves now?"

Raven finished reading a webpage and then gazed at Jordan. "You might have a point. It's made by WT Gaming and Programming – a very small family business in Bury St. Edmunds."

"Suffolk?"

She nodded. "In one."

"We were going to try HiSpec as well," said Jordan.

"Home of a million microprocessors..."

"With a factory in Cambridge," Jordan added.

Raven smiled. "I see where you're going with this. It's not far from Suffolk. It'd be easy to live in Suffolk and commute into Cambridge."

For a moment, Angel paused. Then he turned towards Jordan. "I'll find you another car, but it won't be like the Jag. It'll take time to replace all those microchips and beef up its security, before you get the all-clear to drive it again. For now," he said, "take the rest of the day off. It's a weekend and you look terrible."

WT Gaming and Programming was named after the joint owners: the Warner twins. Ian and Neil were wearing identical smart but casual clothes, identical spectacles and identical heavily gelled hairstyles. They were obviously doing their best to confuse people. It also made them funny and sinister at the same time. Jordan could have been talking to one man standing next to a full-length mirror, except that they seemed to take it in turns to speak.

"We don't have a big crew," Ian told him.

"Big isn't necessary," said Neil in an identical accent.

"Good is more important," Ian continued. "We have few but good people."

"But you did have a problem with SetLink," Jordan said.

They nodded and glanced at each other. Ian replied, "When you phoned and said you'd got some information about a hacking incident, we were..."

"Intrigued," Neil put in.

"Yes, intrigued. That's why we agreed to see you."

Both twins turned their uncanny gaze on him, as if they expected Jordan to tell them everything he knew. But he knew very little. He'd bluffed his way into WT Gaming and Programming. "First, I want to ask you something," Jordan said.

"Do you now?"

"Did you find out who hacked into Cockenzie's SetLink?"

"Sort of," Ian answered warily.

"He came to us," Neil explained.

Jordan nodded. "And you gave him a job?"

"We might've done."

"What's his name?"

"Why do you want to know?"

Jordan shifted his approach. "Is he here now?"

The twins hesitated.

"That means yes," Jordan said. "I'd like to have a quick chat."

Half-heartedly, Ian said, "All right. I'll go and get him."

Neil gave his brother a nod.

Jordan suspected that the gesture conveyed more than just agreement but, if he was right, the twins were using a sign language that he didn't understand.

Neil sat down at his desk and gazed at Jordan, but didn't say a word.

Jordan didn't trust the brothers. In the quiet, he adjusted his hearing to maximum. He wanted to find out if Ian and the programmer were talking nearby. He didn't pick up any voices, though. He heard lorries and cars flying past on the A14, various unidentifiable industrial clunks, bangs and squeals coming from the bigger factories on the estate, the wind whooshing around the buildings, a door slamming and footsteps. Someone was running away.

At once, Jordan realized what the twins' look had meant. They'd agreed silently to tip off their employee.

Jordan jumped up. Sarcastically, he said, "Thanks for

your help." He crashed through the door and brushed past Ian, who was no doubt returning to tell Jordan that the man wasn't available after all. Jordan dashed to the exit just in time to see someone jump into an old Vauxhall and slam the door shut. The sound of the engine revving was like the roar of a jet in Jordan's ears. He turned down the volume as he sprinted towards the car.

Weaving its way out of the twisty car park, the Vauxhall could not get up any great speed.

Determined to cut off the worker's retreat, Jordan made for the car park's exit. The Vauxhall slowed to take the final bend and Jordan appeared at the driver's window.

Knowing that the car was about to accelerate away from the estate, Jordan had to make a quick decision. He raised his right arm and punched through the glass.

9 DEEP WEB

Splinters of glass flew everywhere. The driver was so surprised that he yanked on the steering wheel in an attempt to get away from Jordan. The car veered left and crashed into a bollard.

Jordan bent down towards the broken window, watched the airbag deflate like a burst balloon, and said, "In a hurry to get away? That means you've done something bad."

The man at the wheel was about twenty-five. His seat

belt and the airbag had pinned him down, so he wasn't hurt in the low-speed collision. Even so, he seemed incapable of speech. His mouth hung open, but he couldn't form words. He'd been stunned by Jordan's ferocity and the accident.

"What's your name?"

Surrounded by shiny fragments of glass, he struggled to reply, "Dipak Hardikar."

"I know you knocked out a power station in Edinburgh. I want to know what else you've done." Jordan brushed away the remaining beads of glass from the lower edge of the window and then leaned on it with his right forearm.

Dipak shifted his gaze to Jordan's hand. Perhaps he was expecting blood and bruising, but he noticed for the first time that there was something different about Jordan's whole arm. "Nothing," he stammered.

"Nothing? Perhaps you're a bit hazy on the law about misusing computers. If the police take yours away, their specialists will have a field day, looking at what you've done."

He appeared to be recovering from the shock. "They won't find anything."

"I know some experts who will."

"What do you want?"

Jordan looked closely into Hardikar's face as he replied. "I want to know what you've got against Phil Lazenby."

There was no sign of recognition at all. "Who?"

"I want to know why you hacked into an aeroplane's flight system."

"I didn't!"

"Why did you run away? What have you done?"

"Look. I..." He stared down at his lap, littered with glassy diamonds. "I don't know who you are."

"I'm Jordan Stryker and I can turn pretty nasty." He felt like a fraud because he never thought of himself as cruel.

"All right. You see, I'm not supposed to be here. I don't have all the papers to..."

For a few seconds, Jordan didn't realize what Dipak was trying to say. Then he twigged. "Oh. Okay. But if you're an illegal immigrant, how come you've got a driving licence and a car?"

Looking even more guilty, Dipak kept his head bowed. "The car's not mine. It's a friend's."

Two people walking past stopped to get a good look at the accident. Realizing there was only a dent and a broken window, they moved on. The Warner twins gazed out of their unit's window.

Jordan laughed softly. "This is really piling up. I could get you into a mountain of trouble. I could tell the police you're not supposed to be in the country, you're driving without a licence and you go in for a lot of hacking."

"Will you?"

"Yes." He paused for two or three seconds before adding, "Unless you show me every cyber attack you've made this year."

Dipak groaned.

"Do we have a bargain?"

Clearly doubtful, Dipak hesitated.

Jordan took out his mobile and pretended to get ready to make a call.

"All right," said Dipak.

"Back to your place, is it?"

"We can do it here, right now, if you want."

"How come?" Jordan asked.

"I don't keep records on a hard drive. Not safe enough. I hide my stuff in the deep web. I can access it from any computer."

"The deep web? What's that?" Jordan paused and then added, "Don't tell me here. Park the car – if it still goes – and we'll sort it out inside."

* * *

Dipak did not look comfortable in jeans and sweatshirt. Most likely, he would have preferred to wear something more formal, but his circumstances probably prevented it.

As he logged on, he spoke quietly and quickly. "When you surf the internet, that's all you're doing. Surfing. Skimming the surface. You're seeing a tiny percentage of what's really there. There's this huge mass of stuff beyond the reach of normal search engines. It's called the deep web. It's made up of sites that don't work any more, abandoned addresses, online businesses that have gone bust and that sort of thing. Quite a few are military sites from the early days of the internet – long since dumped and replaced by more secure technology. People like me dive down into it, drag up a dead site, revive it to do what we want and then sink it again. No one's any the wiser. Back down in the depths, nobody else is going to come across it. It's a drop of water in a great big ocean."

"Handy."

"Yes. There's a lot of information down there. Lots of data and details of people's lives in discarded sites. If you want someone else's identity, there's plenty to choose from. Lots of passwords as well. When people replace a website, they often keep the same password."

"So you go fishing for it?"

"Exactly. Loads of spam comes from dead addresses. And the deep web is where you'll find horrid sites as well." He pulled a face and said, "You can guess the sort of thing."

Jordan began to warm to Dipak. He was keen, clear and convincing. No doubt he was a good hacker, but Jordan could not assume that he was as harmless as he seemed. Jordan had to continue playing the part of a bully. He had to remain suspicious.

"There you are," Dipak said, waving at the monitor. "It looks like a site for an old netball team. It is. But the team disbanded years ago. Now, I use the fixture list to log all my online activities. The results speak for themselves. A win's where I broke in. A defeat's where I didn't get past security."

"What's a draw?"

"I didn't get in, but there's at least one loophole still to try. Look," he said as he scrolled down, "there's that Scottish power station. Cockenzie. A win."

Jordan nodded, but concentrated on the fixture list. On Monday 5th March – the date of the Edinburgh aeroplane crash – Dipak's log showed that he was trying to muscle his way into the Indian government's website. Last night, at the moment when Jordan's car began to move mysteriously with its shocked passenger trapped inside, Dipak was wrestling with an online electronic store. The day before, when Victoria Truman's high-tech home went up in flames, there was no record of what Dipak was doing. When Jordan queried it, Dipak said he was simply on his way home from work.

Jordan knew that Dipak was familiar enough with computers to invent a false log of his activities, but it looked genuine and he'd had no time to fake it. "Have you heard of Forew?" Jordan spelled it out to make sure.

"Yes."

Jordan's heart leaped. "What is it?" He held his breath.

"Shorthand for foreword. You see it a lot on the web."

"Oh." Jordan's anticipation evaporated at once because Raven had already mentioned that.

"Have you seen what you want?" Dipak asked. "No aeroplanes or air traffic control systems."

"I guess so."

Dipak gazed at him. "Are you going to keep your word?"

"Yes," Jordan answered. Then he added a threat. "Unless I find out you haven't been on the level with me."

Dipak nodded towards the screen. "I've shown you everything. Honest. Totally open."

"I hope so," Jordan replied. "I'll leave you to it now. But you've still got some explaining to do."

"What do you mean?"

"You've got to tell your mate what happened to his car."

HiSpec MicroSystems had refused to cooperate. According to Raven, the cagey company was not willing to provide a list of its employees. So Jordan had come up with a different tactic to find out who worked there.

But, standing outside HiSpec's factory on the outskirts of Cambridge, he might have been looking at a fortress or a prison. Even late at night, floodlights blazed all around the premises, illuminating the car park and every approach. Jordan could see two guards in the security block at the front of the main building. Set to maximum, his eyesight picked out closed-circuit TV cameras at every corner. Breaking into the company and stealing a list of its staff suddenly seemed ridiculous and impossible.

Frustrated, he walked away with a sigh.

But he wasn't downhearted for long. He had another

idea for discovering who worked for the electronics giant. All he needed was help from someone like Merrick Breeze or Dipak Hardikar. He chose Dipak.

10 CYBER STORM

On his mobile, Jordan said to Angel, "I'm staying in the Suffolk safe house tonight so I can see a hacker in the morning. He'll get me into HiSpec's files."

"A virtual break-in has its advantages. Was it Raven's idea?"

"No. Mine."

"Can you be sure your hacker's not Short Circuit?" Angel asked.

"Not totally, no. But I don't think so."

"Stay focused, Jordan. Don't drop your guard."

"Okay. But..."

"What?"

"I think I'll have to bribe him to get what I want."

"Bribe him with what?"

"I'm using him because he's an illegal immigrant," Jordan said. "I bet he'll do anything for a British passport or whatever he needs to stay in this country."

"A thousand pounds would be easier."

Jordan replied, "The passport's worth a lot more to him."

"Well..."

"You did it for the new me."

"All right. If he delivers the goods, put all his details into the system – including a mugshot – and I'll pull a few strings. Now," Angel continued, "I've got a couple of jobs for you while you're up there. We never did chase the history of the victims we're sure about. The fire at Victoria Truman's hasn't left anything to go on. So, try a trip to Long Melford. I've cleared you to get into Phil Lazenby's house. Check him out. Including his writing."

"Will there be anyone around?"

"His wife died a few years ago. Two children long since moved out. Not much contact. You've got it to yourself."

"What's the second job?"

"Carlton Reed's wife – Demi – is expecting you tomorrow in Woodbridge. Around lunchtime. I've put a briefing and cover story for you on the system. Along with Phil Lazenby's address."

On Tuesday morning, Dipak's car limped into the parking area. Part of the bumper was held in place with duct tape. The driver's window was an ill-fitting piece of transparent plastic. It was attached to the door with haphazard pieces of tape, like an ineptly bandaged wound.

Jordan intercepted the IT worker before he entered the factory. Together, they stood under the canopy by the front door while rain splashed down, doing its best to penetrate the improvised window of Dipak's car.

Jordan said, "I want you to do something for me."

Dipak frowned. "What's that?"

"You'll have heard of HiSpec MicroSystems."

"Of course."

"Well, I need a list of people who work there."

"Who are you?"

"I told you. Jordan Stryker."

"Yes, but..."

Jordan interrupted. "You could hack into the company and get it for me."

Dipak shook his head. "HiSpec's wrapped up. Plenty have tried, but no one's cracked it."

"Okay. You could hack into the bank that handles the workers' pay."

"It's possible. Some banks aren't as secure as they like to think."

"Good," said Jordan. "It's a deal."

Puzzled, Dipak asked, "If it's a deal, what do I get out of it?"

"I'm coming to that," Jordan told him, "but there's something else first. A bank's only going to pay people who work there now. It'd be good to find out who's worked for them in the last five years, or whatever. Can you dredge up old lists from the deep web?"

Dipak sighed. "Maybe."

"Really, I'm after anything you can get on HiSpec workers."

"I could try, but..."

Rain pelted Bury St. Edmunds, turning the car park into a shallow pool. Above them, water gushed along the gutter.

"If you give me what I want, I'll get you a British passport."

Dipak's eyes shone suddenly. "Really?"

Jordan nodded.

"How can I be sure?"

"You can't, but I kept my word yesterday. I will this time as well."

Dipak looked into Jordan's face for a few seconds, assessing his truthfulness.

Jordan said, "Even if you're not sure about me, it's worth a gamble, isn't it?"

"Yes."

Jordan smiled. "I thought so, but I'll do what I've promised – if you give me what I need."

"How do I get stuff to you?"

Jordan gave Dipak an e-mail address. "And make sure you attach a passport-style photo," he said. Then he pulled his collar up around his neck and made a dash for his car.

One wide road ran through the Suffolk village of Long Melford. On either side, every other shop seemed to sell antiques. Guided by his inertial navigation system, Jordan drove into a quiet lane just off the main road and parked outside Phil Lazenby's deserted house. It was a modest bungalow with a small neat lawn and sculptured hedge that must have been tended by a gardener during the pilot's frequent absences. When Jordan went through the gate at the side of the property, he could see that the back garden was also immaculate. Someone had banished every single weed from the flower beds.

The house key was where Angel said it would be – under the large pot by the back door. Jordan used it to let himself into the kitchen. Apart from the purring of the fridge-freezer, the place was silent. Eerie really. And immensely sad.

Jordan took a deep breath and went into the tiny lobby. By the front door, a few letters had fallen untidily onto the floor. They would never be opened and answered by Captain Lazenby. Jordan walked into the living room. At first glance, there wasn't much in it. A settee and comfy chair, a coffee table, a TV, a wood-burning stove with a small stack of logs, and very little furniture apart from a writing desk. At once, Jordan made for it.

On the desk, there was a space that would probably have been occupied by a laptop, but it wasn't there. On the left, there were various computer CDs, a printer, a radio-controlled clock, a notepad, photographs of his wife and children, and a stack of paper. On the right, seven large folders were propped up on a shelf. Jordan took the middle one and opened it at a random page. It contained rows and rows of old dull postage stamps. Alongside every one, there was a neatly handwritten note about the stamp: its designer, subject and date of issue. Turning the pages, Jordan realized that he was looking at a bulky stamp collection. All of the ones in this album seemed to be from the Netherlands. He had no idea if the collection was valuable or worthless. Uninterested and disappointed, he closed the folder and put it back on its shelf.

He couldn't see a diary, so instead he examined the notepad. Flicking through it, he saw phone numbers, an old list of Christmas gifts, a note about something in Ipswich, a record of jobs that needed doing around the house, and a message about a flight to Amsterdam. The pilot's handwriting was large and precise. Jordan was hardly an expert on grammar, but he couldn't see a single spelling mistake. Plainly, the jottings were not the work of someone who was dyslexic. The word Captain Lazenby had written on the back of Paige Ottaway's photo would not have been a misspelling.

Jordan reached for the pictures of Mrs. Lazenby and the couple's children. He slipped them out of their frames, turned them over and let out a sigh. The pilot had not jotted anything on the backs.

It really didn't matter if Jordan left the photos and

frames scattered on the desk, but he reassembled them anyway. Somehow, that seemed more respectful.

When he'd finished putting everything back as it had been, he looked again at one of the notepad pages. Phil had written three lines.

Ipswich 28/4
How many dealers?
Good Colombian and Dutch?

Jordan wasn't certain what it meant, but an idea formed in his mind. He put down the pad and went on a slow walk around the rest of the house. He checked every drawer in the bedrooms just in case there was a diary or anything else that might shed more light on Captain Lazenby – and why someone might want to kill him. But nothing grabbed Jordan's attention.

As soon as Jordan entered Demi Reed's living room in Woodbridge, he noticed the bass guitar propped up in one corner. Around its neck was hung a large gold crucifix. Jordan took one look at the shrine and realized at once why he'd heard of Carlton Reed. Until Short Circuit had put an end to his life, Carlton had been a musician, the bassist in a group called Cyber Storm.

Demi noticed his gaze and said, "God claimed a good man. Did you know Carlton? I mean, his music?"

Jordan nodded. "I downloaded the first album. It's such a shame."

"Amen." Demi sat down heavily and waved Jordan towards another chair.

The room was the opposite of Captain Lazenby's. It was packed with furniture and untidy. Every surface seemed to be covered in magazines, mugs, leaflets, CDs and trinkets.

"Was he touring in Ecuador?"

"They'd been all over South America," Demi replied. "You see, there's no money in selling recorded music these days. It's all about playing live. He was away on tour a lot. Too much. But I'll tell you this. He never missed being here for our daughter's birthday. Except for the year he did jury service. And when he went back to Jamaica because his parents got caught up in the hurricane. He couldn't help either of those. He loved his family. That's the sort of man he was."

Jordan was wondering if it was a coincidence that Carlton's group was called Cyber Storm when Short Circuit was summoning electronic disasters. "How did the band get its name?" he asked.

She shrugged. "It sounded good. There's strength in the combination of the man-made – that's the cyber part – and an act of God. That's what I think, anyway."

Jordan took three photographs out of his pocket and spread them over the clutter on the coffee table.

Watching him, Demi said, "Ah, yes. A policeman told me you were looking into disturbances on the plane. Like drinking too much. Well, I'll tell you now, that wasn't Carlton's scene. He never touched a drop. Except when... Anyway, it wasn't him."

Jordan pointed to the images of Victoria Truman, Phil Lazenby and Paige Ottaway. "These people were caught up in it. I wanted to know if Carlton knew any of them, but..." He looked at her. "Sorry, but I've got to ask you instead."

Demi put her head on one side as she examined the pictures. Then she pushed away the photos of the two women. "I don't know them." Tapping the other one, she added, "But him..."

"Yes?" Jordan prompted.

"He's familiar."

"Captain Phil..."

"Got it!" she interrupted. "He's that hero pilot. The one who's just died. God bless him. If you ask me, it's ironic. He walked away from a plane crash, but a bump in a car got the better of him. The Lord works in mysterious ways."

Disappointed, Jordan asked, "You never met him? Phil Lazenby, that is."

"No." She raised her eyes to the ceiling and said, "I've never met Him, either. But one day...when I'm with Carlton again."

To Jordan, she seemed open, honest and deeply wounded by her husband's death.

"Did he know anyone heavily into electronics?"

"Yes. The band's manager, the sound engineers, the special effects crew..."

"Sorry. Silly question." Jordan wiped the smile from his face and took a deep breath, "Did the group do drugs?"

She sat upright and stared at Jordan. "God help me, no. No drink and no drugs. Except... Not the sort you mean anyway. I'll tell you this. He had terrible migraines. He was always taking something for them. That's all."

"Just one more thing. Did he know Lemon Jelly, the group?"

She thought for a moment and then answered, "Yes. I mean, he wouldn't have known them if they'd walked into church, but he knew of them. We've got their CDs somewhere. Or maybe Carlton downloaded their stuff. Anyway, they used a lot of samples."

Jordan nodded. "Like a man talking about all the places he's been to?"

Demi's face lit up. "Yes, I remember that one. I don't know what it's called – I'm hopeless with titles – but I can hear it right now. In my head. I used to say that man's travelled as much as Carlton." She laughed at the memory.

"Yeah," Jordan replied. "I like it as well."

As he left, Jordan made a decision to visit another address in Suffolk. Eager to find out why Captain Lazenby had chosen to write his curious note on Paige Ottaway's photograph, he drove towards Felixstowe.

11 BRICK WALL

In his mind, Jordan searched the internet for information on Paige Ottaway. Her name cropped up all over the place. From 2006 to 2010, she'd been chairwoman of her local Women's Institute. She'd worked as a volunteer for several charities and she'd been a Suffolk councillor for a while. Yet the world outside her own area hadn't taken any notice of her. She'd become newsworthy only when she died in a freak accident during a brain operation. At least, all the reports called it an accident.

The man who answered Jordan's knock on the door seemed too young to be Mrs. Ottaway's partner. Jordan said, "Hello. Is this where Paige Ottaway lived?"

The man in the doorway looked puzzled, but nodded. "I'm her son. What do you want?"

"A chat about her operation and what went wrong."

"Who are you?"

"Jordan Stryker. I'm looking into a few accidents like your mum's."

Paige's son sucked in a sharp breath. "A few?"

Jordan nodded.

"You're a bit young."

"I still care," Jordan replied.

"All right. You'd better come in. I'm Sam, by the way."

In the living room of the small terraced house, Jordan asked, "Is your dad in?"

"No. I don't know where he is. Since Mum died, he's been going downhill fast. Who knows what he's up to? Doing more crazy things, I dare say. Anyway, what are you doing here? What's it all about?"

Reaching into his pocket, Jordan replied, "I've got some photos." While he spread them out, he named each of the people. "Phil Lazenby, Victoria Truman and Carlton Reed."

Sam gazed at the portraits for a few seconds and then looked up at Jordan. "I don't know them, but the first one's that pilot. Have the other two died in accidents as well?"

"Yes."

"Captain Lazenby was in a car, not a hospital. What about the other two?"

"A plane crash and a house fire."

"What have they got to do with Mum, then?" asked Sam.

"They're from round here and their problems all kicked off with an electrical fault."

"What are you trying to say?"

"What if it was sabotage?"

Sam's mouth opened. "What? What do you mean? Who'd do that? It doesn't make sense. Why are you talking about sabotage?"

Jordan decided to change direction. "What sort of person was your mum?"

Still looking bemused, Sam replied, "A pillar of the community, as they say. She'd do anything for anybody. She helped out with the homeless, alcoholics, immigrants, the elderly. All that sort of thing. Everyone around here knew her. No one would...you know...do what you're suggesting."

"Okay," Jordan said, sensing that he couldn't push Sam Ottaway much further.

"I've just been talking to a solicitor. She thinks we've got a chance of suing the hospital for negligence. Negligence, not on purpose. That's why I'm here – to tell Dad. A case like that'd give him a focus. He'd feel like someone was paying him attention for a change."

The phone rang. With a glance at Jordan, Sam answered it. "Hello? Sam Ottaway." He listened to the voice for a few seconds and then said, "Yes, that's right." Another gap before he exclaimed, "He's what?" He sighed and shook his head. "All right. I'm on my way. I'll be there in five. Or less." He slammed down the phone and said, "I've got to go to the hospital. It's Dad."

"What's wrong?"

Sam grabbed a coat. "He's chained himself to the railings as some sort of protest or stunt. But he's ill."

"Maybe I can help," said Jordan.

"I don't know how," Sam replied as he made for the door. "But I can't stop you following me."

It was a strange sight. Mr. Ottaway was propped against a low brick wall outside the hospital and his arm was bent back. Heavy-duty handcuffs attached one wrist to the tall iron railings that were embedded in the mortar. He looked like a schoolboy with his hand up, wanting to go to the toilet. But he was also unconscious and a pale blue colour. A doctor was pushing awkwardly and repeatedly on his chest. Even though the wall was squat, Mr. Ottaway's arm wasn't long enough to allow the doctor to place him flat on the ground. Hospital staff had erected a large sheet to stop everyone peering at the scene. Frustrated, the doctor called out, "Where's the fire engine? They're supposed to be bringing cutting gear."

"What's happened?" Sam asked. "I'm his son."

"Cardiac arrest," the doctor panted. "He'd be okay if I could get him inside."

A nurse said, "There's a DIY store a couple of minutes down the road."

The doctor nodded. "Get us a hacksaw."

Jordan was not going to wait. The sheet was like a screen. It hid him from any photographers. He clambered onto the wall and took the metal upright in both hands. It felt solid and immovable, but he didn't let that put him off. Summoning all his strength, he tried to wrench it out of the mortar by yanking it upwards. It didn't budge. Instead, he tried twisting it.

No one else thought he stood a chance, so they ignored him.

His false hand gripped the metal tightly and he slowly increased the torque. Below, the grey mortar that topped the bricks began to show tiny cracks. Encouraged, Jordan tried sudden jerks, one after the other, until he could feel some give in the fixing. As the metal rod began to move, it rattled against Mr. Ottaway's handcuff.

Sam and a nurse with a hospital stretcher stared in surprise as Jordan continued to loosen the railing.

The doctor didn't pay Jordan any attention. He was becoming more and more concerned. And frustrated. "I'm going to lose him if we don't get him in soon!"

Jordan twisted the upright through a small angle, first one way and then the other, grinding the mortar into powder. It fell like ash from the wall onto Mr. Ottaway and the doctor. Even the wall below began to give way under his relentless pressure. A few bricks shifted.

Against the odds, the railing broke free of the wall and everyone except Mr. Ottaway looked up. At once, Mr. Ottaway's manacled hand fell to his side.

The doctor didn't waste any time. "The stretcher!" he shouted. "Let's go."

Jordan was still standing on the wall with the warped railing in his hand when the staff sped to the entrance with their patient, followed by Sam Ottaway. The last sight he saw with terahertz vision was Mr. Ottaway's feet overhanging the stretcher. Between his shoes and his socks was hidden a small key. It was almost certainly the key that operated the handcuff. Jordan shook his head and wished he'd seen it before.

In the waiting room, Sam glanced at Jordan and said, "Thanks for what you did out there. I didn't think... Anyway, you did it."

Being in a hospital brought back all sorts of harrowing memories for Jordan. Tilting his head towards the emergency room, he asked, "Have you heard anything?"

"Not a lot. But a nurse said he'd be okay now."

"Good." Jordan hesitated before adding, "Just one more thing."

"What?"

"Do you know why anyone would write Forew on the back of a photo of your mum?"

"Forew?"

Jordan nodded. "Maybe her photo was just the handiest piece of paper, but maybe it was something to do with her."

Sam shook his head. "Doesn't mean a thing to me."

"Sure?"

"Certain," Sam answered. "When Dad's...*if* he's all right, I'll ask him as well."

"Okay. Thanks."

"Let me know if you turn anything up," Sam said, "but I think you're wasting your time."

With her mouth full, Kate Stelfox said, "I bet Raven doesn't stuff her face like this."

Jordan was sitting with her in Unit Red's engineering workshop. He shrugged as he bit into his own pie.

Kate wiped away the trickle of brown sauce from the side of her mouth with an oil-stained hand. "She's got the figure of a supermodel living on lettuce. Awesome."

"Maybe that's why she's a good agent."

"How come?"

"No one can see her when she's standing sideways," Jordan said. "And she's thin enough to walk through the narrowest gaps."

Built more for strength than elegance, Kate smiled. "Actually, she's more slim than thin."

Jordan looked puzzled. "There's a difference?"

"Thin sounds unhealthy. Slim sounds elegant." Changing the subject, Kate said, "Have you seen the press coverage of Captain Lazenby? I didn't know Unit

Red's got such power over what gets out there and what doesn't. Anyway, it's the first officer in the Edinburgh crash that I noticed. That's what we're supposed to call a co-pilot these days, I think." She glanced down at her newspaper. "He talks up Phil Lazenby, says he's deeply upset by what's happened and then throws this in. 'As much as I admire what the captain did – and he did a great job – the heroics weren't a one-man show. All the flight crew did their bit. That's why every passenger got out safely.'" Kate gazed at Jordan. "He doesn't think it's right he's been left out of the award ceremonies."

"I suppose it's worth checking him out. He must know quite a bit about electronics."

"It'd be interesting if he had something against the other victims as well, wouldn't it?"

"What's his name?"

"Toby Cotterill," Kate answered.

"I've been wondering about something else. Do you think being a pilot would be a good cover for drug dealing?"

"What makes you ask?" Kate said, popping in another piece of pie.

"Phil Lazenby wrote something on a pad. *How many dealers? Good Colombian and Dutch?* I just thought…"

Kate nodded. "I see what you mean. I don't suppose

pilots get as many security checks as passengers, but I don't really know."

"Demi Reed said Carlton didn't have anything to do with drugs, but she would, wouldn't she? She said he didn't do a lot of other things – apart from the exceptions when he did."

Kate put her lunch aside and took a drink. "You're wondering if they were all into drugs, one way or another."

"Yeah, but I can't see Victoria Truman as a dealer. She could hardly get out of her house, according to the neighbours."

"How about a receiver?" Kate asked.

"What?"

"Maybe she was in pain. Maybe something like cannabis helped. It's not unheard of."

"I see what you mean," Jordan said. "But there's no house left to search." Deprived of an obvious way forward, he waved his left hand towards the Jaguar. "How's it going?"

"Good. Ahead of schedule. You'll get it back sooner than Angel thinks."

Toby Cotterill lived near Kempton Park Racecourse in Sunbury, between the Thames and the M3. No doubt, it was convenient for Heathrow. But there was no answer when Jordan pressed the bell push. He rang again. After a couple of minutes, he gave up and walked slowly around the detached house. He detected no sound and no movement. But he noticed that the curtains were drawn in one downstairs room and an upstairs window was slightly open.

He turned on his terahertz vision and peered towards the curtained window. He saw a rubber plant on the windowsill and the shape of furniture beyond, but there was too great a distance between the curtain and the rest of the room to make out details. He was puzzled by the profile of an armchair, though. There was a bump at the top that looked exactly like someone's head.

Jordan was eager to discover if Captain Lazenby's co-pilot had any connection with Short Circuit's other victims, but he didn't want to break through the front door when there was a possibility that someone was inside, refusing to answer the doorbell. He had to be more subtle. He went back to his car, changed his shoes and put on his special gloves. It was time to see if super-grip technology worked. It was time to walk up a wall.

The shoes made normal walking slightly odd. With each footfall, he could feel himself sticking to the pavement. Yet, when he lifted each foot, the nanotechnology fibres peeled away from the paving. It was like walking on a thin layer of glue.

He stopped in the back garden and looked towards the open window. It was a long way up. More concerning, it was a long way down onto the concrete patio if the microscopic Velcro lost its grip.

He checked that the fastenings on his shoes were firm and that the tight-fitting gloves were secure. Then he began.

Getting started was difficult. Not physically difficult. With both hands and one foot attached to the wall, it was a mental challenge to trust the technology enough to lift his other foot. His instinct told him that gravity would take over and he would fall. His brain told him that some unknown scientist had tested the technology over and over again. He would be safe. Sheer willpower made him lift his right foot and place it flat on the brickwork. And there he was. Like an enormous four-legged spider attached to the bottom of the wall. He glanced upwards. The window seemed far away.

He tore his left hand off the wall, reached up as high as he dared and reattached it. Then he did the same in turn with his artificial hand, his left foot and his right foot. It was incredibly slow, but he had progressed by four layers of bricks.

Taking a deep breath, he did the same again and found himself at the height of the downstairs windows.

Toby's garden had high hedges so, for the moment, Jordan's bizarre antics would go unseen. As he got higher, he would become more visible. He had to hope that he wouldn't be spotted. He tried to convince himself that nobody would glance upwards to check if a boy was clinging to the outside wall of a house.

He could hardly believe what he was doing. It was crazy, unnerving and unnatural. He was also surprised by the sudden aches and tension in his body. He had hardly got going and already he felt as if he was tearing his muscles. As he mounted another metre, he guessed why the climb was sapping his strength so quickly. He was human, not a spider, and his muscles weren't designed for this sort of activity. Hauling himself slowly up the brick wall was exhausting.

At least he was winning the battle against the feeling that he was about to plunge from the vertical surface. Even so, he knew that mountain climbers always attached ropes to themselves in case the worst happened. Jordan did not have ropes or a safety net.

He stretched out again, one limb at a time, and lurched awkwardly upwards. He was now beyond the point when looking down was a good idea. He kept his eyes on the bricks right in front of him and looked up to the window after every step, willing it closer. The cool wind seemed stronger at this height. Unsettling him, it swept between his body and the wall.

Twice more, he reached out, arched his back and then hunched up. His movement reminded him of a worm's – slowly elongating and scrunching up in sequence – instead of a speedy spider's progress. He might have moved more efficiently if he'd had sticky kneepads instead of shoes.

If he'd had the time to practise and gain confidence with the super-grip clothing, it would probably have been fun to scuttle up walls and across ceilings. Right now, though, he was neither practised nor confident. He wasn't scared because he felt firmly attached to the brickwork, but it had not yet become fun.

He could put out an arm and grasp the windowsill now, but he wanted to approach the opening from the side. Peeling each point of contact carefully from the wall one-by-one, he moved a step to the right and another step upwards until he was alongside the window.

He lifted his left hand from the wall and pushed the window open further, but it came to a sudden stop. The gap was far too narrow for him to slip through. That was probably the idea. No doubt it was a safety feature to stop outsiders getting in and anyone inside falling out.

Having got this far, Jordan was not going to turn back. He anchored his left hand to a brick, twisted uncomfortably, and grabbed the window in his right hand. Steeling himself – hoping that the three remaining contact points were enough – he powered up his arm and forced the window back. Something metallic in the mechanism grated and then snapped, and the window opened wide, welcoming him into Toby Cotterill's home.

He tore his gloved hand from the window frame and slunk sideways. Attaching his shoes to the inside windowsill, he ducked down and slipped into an empty bedroom. Out of the wind and no longer needing to defy gravity, he breathed a sigh of relief and eased himself quietly onto the floor. As he crept towards the door, his shoes lifted the fitted carpet a little, like a vacuum cleaner sucking at the fibres.

He went out onto the landing and made for the stairs. Just as he was about to go down, he froze. He heard a voice from somewhere downstairs. A threatening voice.

Jordan was in too deep to withdraw now. Keeping his breathing deliberately quiet and tiptoeing down the wooden staircase, he descended into the hall. One door was closed. It probably led to the kitchen because the other three were open and he could see into a bathroom, the darkened living room and a dining room. Instinct made him head for the living room, made shadowy by drawn curtains.

The door was not wide open. Jordan could not see much through the narrow angle. But he gasped when he saw a man in his underwear tied to an armchair. He had a gag across his mouth and something like a plant pot beside his legs. He was looking down at the container with an expression of fear on his face.

12 SHOCK WAVE

Jordan flattened himself against the wall, staying out of sight. Using his brain/computer interface, he logged on and quickly completed a search of the web. *Toby Cotterill; pilot; Edinburgh.* In his online mind, the top result was an article on the aeroplane that ditched in the Forth. It included a picture of the triumphant crew. Toby was standing next to Captain Lazenby. Jordan zoomed in. Yes. He recognized the face. The first officer was now captive in his own home, prevented from talking by a bandage tied very tightly over his mouth. And something was terrifying him.

Who was in the living room with him? Was it Short Circuit? How many people were in there? Were they armed? What were they doing and why? Should Jordan crash into the living room in the hope of taking them by surprise? Or should he take a sneaky look first?

He decided that he'd be asking for trouble if he put his head round the door. So, he opted for shock tactics. He would burst into the living room and confront whoever was inside. He steeled himself.

Just as he was about to fly at the door, he heard a voice from the living room.

"Ten minutes more and I'm out of here," it said. "Out of your life. Don't do anything silly and I won't have to sacrifice either of us."

It was a man's voice, not a British accent. *I won't have to sacrifice either of us.* That implied there were only two of them in the room. It also told Jordan that he had a weapon. Jordan frowned. If the unknown man had a knife or a gun, surely he would have said, "Don't do anything silly and I won't have to sacrifice you." So, what sort of weapon did he have? Perhaps something that would kill them both. And why did he say *sacrifice*?

Then it struck Jordan. The intruder could be some sort

of suicide bomber and that package near Toby's feet could well be his home-made bomb.

Jordan's heart leaped. If he was right, he was about to tangle with another bomb. He'd had more than enough of them for a lifetime. He just had to close his eyes to remember how he had been maimed by one explosion. He could see the collapse of his bedroom, the window shattering and broken glass hurtling towards him. He could see his right arm tearing apart. Even now, the thought haunted him. It brought him out in a sweat.

But Jordan couldn't back out now. The feeling of dread didn't change his mind. His plan was still to burst into the room, but his focus would be on that plastic pot. He took a deep breath and threw himself at the door. He dived towards the container and grabbed it with his bionic hand.

Toby looked astounded. Opposite him, sitting on a chair, an unshaven man jumped with shock. Recovering quickly, he reached out for a remote control on the coffee table beside him.

Convinced that he was holding an improvised bomb, Jordan drew back his robotic arm and tried to fling the container out of the door. But it didn't fly anywhere. The device clung to the sticky glove.

The terrorist – or whatever he was – pushed a key on his remote.

Jordan braced himself, but nothing happened.

Taken by surprise, the man fiddled with the remote, probably resetting it.

Jordan wrenched the bomb away from his right hand with his left. Now it was firmly attached to his other hand. In that instant, he knew that, if it went off, he'd lose his real arm. Minimum.

The bomber began to smile. He was gloating. He delayed the detonation to enjoy the strange sight of Jordan's dilemma.

Jordan peeled off the left-hand glove with his false fingers and wrapped it round the pot. With his real hand bare, he could now throw the device. He'd never been any good with that arm, though, so it wouldn't go far and it wouldn't be accurate.

The intruder had had enough amusement. He decided it was time to press the button. And this time he wasn't going to make a mistake.

Jordan lobbed the container behind the large sofa and flung himself to the ground.

The deafening noise of the blast was followed immediately by the shock wave. The windows shattered. Curtains ripped and flailed. Pictures flew off the walls.

Furniture collapsed. Toby was hurled sideways along with the armchair. The TV exploded. The heavy sofa lunged at Jordan. The ceiling lifted momentarily. Pulverized by the explosion, clouds of plaster filled the air.

The bomb took only a couple of seconds to destroy much of the room, but time appeared to slow. Jordan saw it all at reduced speed. His right arm came up protectively in front of him and deflected the settee. The remote control seemed to hover in the air while the man who had activated it was thrust forward against a broken cabinet.

The first to recover his wits, Jordan scrambled towards Toby. "Are you all right?" he asked, tearing off the pilot's gag.

Clearly confused, Toby replied, "Can't hear."

Jordan shouted, "Are you okay?"

Toby took a deep breath and then coughed violently. "I think so. Sort of."

The armchair was shredded. It had taken the force of the blast and probably saved the pilot.

Toby looked around. "My house!" he cried. Still frightened, he added, "What about...?"

The room was fogged with particles of plaster. Even Jordan struggled to see through it, but he detected the bomber's heat signature in the infrared. He was sprawled across the floor on the far side. Picking his way over to him, Jordan saw glass from the cabinet door protruding from his neck and an extraordinary volume of blood. In a loud voice, Jordan said, "He's out of it. Dead."

Jordan wished that he was standing over Short Circuit. He wished that he'd just concluded his second mission. But it wasn't over. This man's methods were nothing like Short Circuit's cyber terrorism.

"What's this all about?" Jordan asked as he clambered over the wreckage and began to untie Toby. "Do you know?"

The pilot clicked into gear. "What time is it?"

"About half past two." Jordan loosened enough cord to free Toby's left arm.

The pilot looked down at his wrist. "Two twenty-six. We've got four minutes before take-off!"

"What?"

"There were two of them. The other one's exactly like me. Could be my double. He took my pilot's licence, clothes and ID. He's had flying lessons. He's posing as me. He's going to kill the pilot and crash the plane into the Houses of Parliament!"

"Are you sure?"

"Yes." Toby nodded towards the bomber. "He was

revelling in it. On a high about what they were doing."

Jordan undid the remaining knot.

"He smashed my landline and mobile," Toby said, unravelling himself from the loops of rope. "Give me yours. Quick. I've got to stop that flight."

Jordan handed over his phone.

Almost at once, Toby looked crestfallen. "I don't know the number!"

"What number?"

"Airport security. I've got it on speed-dial. I don't need to remember it." He glanced at his watch again. Panicking, he yelled, "That flight's always on schedule. They're about to take off!"

A crowd of neighbours had assembled on the lawn outside. One or two were brave enough to approach the front, but they probably thought no one was at home. They might even think they'd seen Toby leaving earlier.

Jordan reclaimed his phone and keyed in his emergency number again. "I know someone who can help. Is it going from Heathrow?"

Toby nodded. "Flight BA460 for Madrid. Terminal 3."

"What's the problem?" Angel asked in Jordan's ear.

"You've got to stop Flight BA460 from Heathrow to Madrid. Two-thirty. One of the pilots isn't who he says he is. He's going to crash the plane in London. On Parliament."

"What? Okay. I trust you. I'll get on to the airport. Stop it first, ask questions later."

Jordan ended the brief call. He could just make out a distant siren. No doubt one of the locals had called the emergency services to the scene of the explosion.

"Is that it?" Toby asked.

Jordan nodded. "My...friend will sort it out."

"Really?"

"Yes."

Toby looked blank. "Who are you?"

Jordan shrugged. "It doesn't matter. But..."

"What?"

"They'll take you to hospital," Jordan said. "Fix you up. I'd like to have a talk, but I'd rather not be around when the police arrive, if I don't have to be. Best not to mention me, eh? It complicates things. I'll visit you in about an hour. Okay?"

"I suppose so. But how do I know the plane...?"

"Watch telly while you're waiting. Hope there's nothing about one coming down on London."

To avoid the swarm of concerned neighbours, Jordan made for the back door.

* * *

Of all the threats to airport security, a terrorist piloting an aeroplane was the scenario that the authorities feared most. Angel did not tell them that his information came from a teenager. He simply activated the coded alert and Heathrow swung into action.

Flight BA460 had left its gate and was taxiing slowly towards the main runway. Allocated a slot, it was in a queue for take-off. It was too risky to recall the aircraft because the rogue pilot would guess that he'd been rumbled. The security staff dreaded what he might do.

They decided to invent a crisis that would allow them to cancel all flights instead of picking on one. Air traffic control announced an immediate airport shutdown. "We have a Boeing 757 turning back for emergency landing with a fuel leak from its right wing. Clear all air traffic. Repeat. Clear all traffic. Return to gates in sequence." To make it look realistic, all of Heathrow's fire appliances raced to the runway and lined up in readiness.

As soon as Flight BA460 pulled up to its gate, it was stormed by specially trained officers. The fake pilot was led away and the authorities set about repairing the chaos to their schedules. Hundreds of disgruntled passengers never got to know that a boy called Jordan Stryker had averted carnage. They knew only hours of disruption to their flights.

* * *

Dodging round patients, visitors and staff, Jordan hurried to Accident and Emergency, where Toby Cotterill had been taken.

Parts of the pilot's arms and legs were sheathed in bandages. His bruised face was patchy blue and his dark hair was still dusted with powdered plaster. He looked like he'd just survived a few rounds with a champion boxer.

Jordan waved a hand towards the television attached to the ceiling. "Have you heard? No crashes on the news. Just a false alarm over an iffy plane and major delays."

Toby nodded.

Jordan waited for a nurse to stride past before pulling up a chair. "I wanted to ask you a few things."

"Fire away," Toby said. "I owe you."

"How did you get on with Captain Lazenby?"

"He's a fine man and a good work colleague. I mean, he *was*."

"That didn't stop you having a go at him in the newspapers."

Toby's battered face took on a red flush. "I hope it didn't come across like that. I was having a go at everyone else, because they treated him like a god and the rest of the crew like we didn't matter. You'd think we were all sitting around having a laugh and a drink while Phil saved our lives. You know, after the Edinburgh incident, I didn't work with him much."

"You fell out?"

"No. We do what our masters tell us. We just didn't get paired up that often."

"Did he have anything to do with drugs?"

Toby raised his eyebrows. "We all do. Our sleep patterns are all over the place. One pill to help us sleep, a different pill to keep us awake. Passengers like their pilots to be awake at the controls."

Jordan smiled. "What about illegal drugs?"

"No chance. He wasn't that sort."

"Where were you when you heard he'd died?"

"In a Paris hotel, watching BBC News, waiting for the sleeping pill to kick in," Toby answered. He shook his head sadly. "News was scrolling across the bottom of the screen. *Hero pilot dies.*"

Jordan remembered that Paris was the first place mentioned in the Lemon Jelly song. He said, "You get around. Could call you a ramblin' man."

Toby's face creased with puzzlement. "Um... I suppose so."

His reaction was not suspicious. Jordan changed

tactics. "How did you meet Carlton Reed?"

"Who?" Toby said, genuinely mystified.

"Sorry. I thought... Anyway, how about someone or something called Forew?"

Toby shook his head. "You're strange. And I never found out how you got into my house."

"Through a bedroom window." With a wry grin, Jordan added, "I might have damaged it a bit."

"It's not the only damage. I won't press charges of breaking and entering." He pointed at the wall clock and said, "The police are coming to interview me in a few minutes. I guess you'll want to evaporate before they arrive."

Jordan nodded. "I can do without the hassle."

"If I thought for one moment you were a bad guy..."

"I'm not."

"I can tell," Toby replied. "Are you still off the record?"

"It's best, yes."

Smiling, Toby shook his head. "You'd better do your disappearing act, then."

Jordan stood up. "Thanks for the warning," he said. "This time, *you* can have the glory for keeping a planeload of passengers safe."

* * *

"I'm annoyed with you," said Angel.

Jordan knew that Unit Red's chief had a stern side to his nature. He stretched out his arms and asked, "Why? What have I done?"

"You took unauthorized time off your case. You went outside your brief."

For a moment, Jordan didn't get it. Then he laughed. "You mean, saving the Houses of Parliament and a lot of politicians?"

Angel's face finally cracked. "The public will never forgive you."

"They'll never know."

"That's true," Angel replied. "Neither will the passengers. They'll be enjoying Madrid, not realizing how close they were to dying in a disaster." He hesitated before adding, "You did well."

"I got lucky."

"Not as lucky as the MPs," Angel said. "But I'm glad you're getting used to the Unit Red way of doing things."

"How do you mean?"

"Plenty of hard work, quite a bit of danger, a small amount of luck and no credit at all. But up here," he said, tapping the side of his head, "you feel good. Sometimes – like now – very good indeed."

"I'd feel even better if I'd got Short Circuit as well. I'm pretty sure it's not Toby Cotterill. For one thing, he was in Paris when I was in Ipswich with Phil Lazenby. And the bloke with the bomb didn't do things like Short Circuit, did he?"

"No," Angel replied. "We're interrogating his mate – the fake pilot – right now. Leave that angle to me. Kate said you were sniffing out a drug connection."

Jordan shook his head. "No sign of it yet."

But Angel's comment made him think again. He remembered the first line on the pilot's notepad. *Ipswich 28/4*. Using his BCI, he went online and searched on *Ipswich 28th April 2012*. It was a Saturday and there were several events on in the town that day. One in particular caught his eye. There had been a stamp fair. He wasn't sure what happened at a stamp fair, so he logged on to the organizer's site. Apparently, about twenty dealers had turned up to sell collectible postage stamps.

Jordan closed his eyes and sighed.

"What's up?" Angel asked.

"False alarm," Jordan admitted. "Phil Lazenby had a collection of stamps. I saw Dutch ones. Maybe he had Colombian ones in a different folder. I bet he phoned someone about what was on sale at a stamp fair on the twenty-eighth of April. It was stamps, not drugs."

"It's marvellous what you can do with an online brain," said Angel. "Which reminds me. Raven's got something for you. A file's come in from Dipak Hardikar."

"Right," Jordan replied. "I'll go and see her."

13 MADISON FLINT

When Jordan walked into the computer room, Raven twisted round and said, "Oh, it's you."

It wasn't the warmest of welcomes. "Hi," he said. "Dipak's sent me something."

"Yes. An e-mail with an attachment." She threw a mass of black hair over her shoulder. "Want to see it on screen or are you going to do it in your amazing brain?"

Approaching her from the side, Jordan noticed how skinny she was. She would have looked in place strutting down a catwalk. Not really tempted to take a peek at her with terahertz vision, Jordan answered, "The screen's easier."

"Here you go." She twisted the monitor so he could read it easily.

In his e-mail, Dipak explained that he hadn't yet been able to break into the bank that handled HiSpec's finances, but he had found staff details from a five-year-old file buried in the deep web.

Raven asked, "Do you want to open it now?"

"Yes, please."

It was an out-of-date list of HiSpec workers and, at a stroke, Jordan had generated hundreds of suspects. Far too many.

Raven laughed. "You look panic-stricken."

"How many people are on this?"

"613."

Jordan swallowed.

"It's not as bad as you think," Raven told him. "Look. Every name's got a job description. I can eliminate all of the admin, cleaners and low-level staff in general. If Short Circuit's here, he's going to be working on microchip design. He's quite senior."

"Unless being a cleaner is his or her cover," Jordan said.

"Doubtful. Internal security is tight, to say the least. Cameras everywhere. They'd spot a cleaner interfering with design."

"How do you know?"

"Chip manufacturers are well known for obsessing about security. That's why they wouldn't tell us anything about personnel. That's why you had to do it by the back door." Raven looked down at her watch. "It's late. Unit Red asks a lot of us, doesn't it? You have to sacrifice your time because the job always comes first. Anyway, I'll go through it in the morning, then save a filtered version. That'll be more manageable."

"Okay. Thanks," Jordan replied.

Jordan's mind had no real limits. The Unit Red computer system was available to him through a brain implant. Once logged in, he had the World Wide Web in his head. Its images were fed into his optic nerve. When he closed his eyes, he created a dark screen for browsing. His resources were infinite, but his skull felt claustrophobic. When he was online, it was crammed with pictures and information.

Almost everybody else in the Unit Red house was asleep. Lying on his bed, Jordan could make out a guard's slow steady footfall along one of the corridors. In the cemetery outside, shrubs rustled in the wind. Above his head, two birds were walking across the roof. Jordan could pinpoint the sounds. The unseen birds were two-and-a-half metres apart. He could detect the smell of damp fertile earth and growing plants, as well as the last meal cooked in the kitchen. Mixed with the airborne cocktail of chemicals was the faint whiff of oil from the workshop.

On his internal screen, he put up Dipak's unfiltered attachment and executed a search for anyone called Forew. He drew a blank. He scrolled through the list, but discovered nothing of interest and soon got bored. Checking HiSpec's staff would be much easier once Raven had edited out unnecessary names, so he decided to wait. Instead, he opened the document's properties. He was surprised to see that it had been created, modified and accessed today. Perhaps it bore the date of 23rd May 2012 because that was when Raven had received and saved it. Even so, he expected a record of its creation five years previously.

In his mind, he formed an e-mail and sent it to Dipak, thanking him for the file, but asking him to send a fresh copy.

Even though it was after midnight, Dipak must still

have been online because, within three minutes, the second copy arrived. Straight away, Jordan examined the file's properties and found its creation date in 2007. It suggested to Jordan that Raven had already started working on the document, modifying it in some way, before she'd saved it.

Why?

Jordan opened the new attachment side-by-side with the one that Raven had written onto the computer. Using a tool that compared two versions of the same document, he discovered that the new file contained 614 entries. Not 613. The comparison program found the extra record in seconds.

For some reason, Raven had deleted all mention of a microchip designer called Madison Flint.

"It's running like a normal electric car," Kate said as Jordan continued the trial drive of his Jaguar. "We've added a collision avoidance system, but most of the clever stuff's waiting for new microchips. Your special features are only running at about twenty per cent. I've engaged the speed limiter, though. The car always knows where it is – clever thing – and it's got a database of the speed limits on every road in the country, so it keeps you on the right side of the law. You can override it, but let's not risk it today."

"Collision avoidance system?"

"If you drive at that lorry in front – or veer off towards a barrier – the car's radar will detect an imminent collision and slow down – or stop – to avoid it. You could be fast asleep or...whatever. It'd do it automatically. And if something comes at you from the side or behind, it'll take evasive action."

If the collision avoidance system had been fitted earlier, Jordan thought, it would have detected a shop front in Ipswich, slowed down and kept Phil Lazenby safe. But perhaps Short Circuit would have been able to override that mechanism too.

"What about me? You're getting new chips for the car – ones that Short Circuit can't attack – but what about the ones in my head and arm?"

Kate shook her head. "I asked. They're too specialized and too complicated to replace in a few days. We can't do anything in the short term. You're going to have to catch him before he can do you any damage."

Jordan eased off the accelerator, pulled over and stopped the car. On their left was an old abandoned industrial site. The nearest building was a large Victorian workhouse. All of its windows had long since fallen out and great cracks had appeared in its walls, as if a giant hand – or an earthquake – had shaken it to death. The place was surrounded by a sturdy wire fence and signs declared, *Danger – Keep Out*.

"Is something wrong?" Kate asked.

"No. Well, yes," Jordan replied, turning off the engine. "I mean, not with the car. But there's something wrong, yes."

"What?"

Jordan glanced at the dashboard. "Are there any bugs in here?"

"Bugs?"

"Listening devices," Jordan explained.

"Oh. Sorry," said Kate. "I'm still a firefighter and engineer at heart. Not used to the spying jargon. No. Not as far as I know."

"Can I tell you something in secret? Something that mustn't get back to Unit Red."

Kate nodded. "Of course. I'm a human being first, not just one of Angel's servants."

"All right." Jordan took in and let out a breath. "Last week, you said Raven's on our side. But what do you really know about her?"

Kate raised her eyebrows. "She's part of Unit Red. Chosen by Angel. Trusted by Angel. That's a good start."

Kate looked sideways at him. "I've got no reason to question Angel's judgement."

"My mum used to say, 'If you question nothing, you learn nothing'."

"I think we're lucky to have Raven. What's bothering you?"

Jordan told Kate what had happened the previous day. He told her about Dipak's document and the deleted information.

"Well..." Kate shook her head. "You're right. It's a bit weird, but let's not jump to conclusions."

"There's only one conclusion to jump to," Jordan replied. "Raven removed someone called Madison Flint from the list."

"But we don't know why. Did you do any more research?"

"Yeah. I found two people called Madison Flint. One of them's young."

"How young?" Kate asked.

"Last year she went on a TV talent show, singing and dancing. She did pretty well for a nine-year-old."

"So, she was four when the HiSpec list came out. What about the other one?"

"She's a Scottish MP so there's lots of information about her."

"And?"

"She's always lived in Scotland. She studied history at university and never had a job in electronics."

"That's all?"

Jordan nodded. "A dead end."

Kate thought for a moment and then said, "You could ask Raven what's going on."

"That'd be like accusing her of something."

"Okay. How about consulting Angel?"

"Even worse. Before I do anything in Unit Red, like talk to Angel or fish around for information about Raven, I want to find out more about Madison Flint. What do you think?"

"Sounds sensible. But how?"

Jordan smiled weakly. "I know someone who'll dig around for me." He started the engine with a thought and a password.

"Yes, my contact's getting you a passport," Jordan said into his mobile. "A real one, not a fake. He's about to go ahead, but he'd be impressed – and get it sorted quicker – if you drag up some more information for us."

"On what?" Dipak asked.

"Some people this time."

"Give me names and a definite reference point – like an address, age, or where they work – and I'll find out everything you'd want to know." He hesitated before admitting, "I only failed once. That was with someone called Jordan Stryker."

"You tried to look me up, then. Bad idea. No. Try Madison Flint instead. She's a bit of a mystery, but she used to work for HiSpec. Maybe still does."

"Madison Flint. All right. It won't take long. I'll let you know."

"Thanks," Jordan replied. "When you've got something, can you call me?"

"All right."

"It's just that I'm having a security issue with e-mails at the moment." Really, he didn't want Raven to see that he was checking out Madison Flint.

"You said you wanted data on people, not a person."

"Yes," Jordan replied. "I'd be very interested if there's any document in the deep web that links Phil Lazenby, Victoria Truman, Carlton Reed and Paige Ottaway."

"Hang on. I didn't get all those names down."

"I'm e-mailing them to you," said Jordan.

"All right. I'll do my best. You're sure I'm getting a genuine British passport?"

"Certain."

* * *

Angel held a hurried and urgent meeting in the bunker. He gazed in turn at Jordan, Raven and Kate. "I've just found out that, a few minutes before Victoria Truman's place burned down last Friday, something else happened in Sudbury."

"What's that?" Jordan asked.

"A judge called Edward Jackson died."

"How?"

"This is the interesting part of the post-mortem." Angel glanced down at his monitor and read, "The software of his pacemaker was hijacked and maliciously reprogrammed to administer destructive shocks to the heart."

For a moment, they all glanced at each other in silence.

"Sounds like Short Circuit to me," Angel said.

No one in the room was going to disagree with him.

Jordan looked at Raven. "That's not in the same league as bringing a plane down."

She shrugged. "If the post-mortem's right and the pacemaker got reprogrammed, it's a lot harder than just stopping it – or killing a circuit or two in a plane."

Kate muttered, "A judge, a pilot, a charity worker,

a musician and a disabled pensioner. Why?"

It was then that Jordan remembered something. He told them, "Demi Reed said Carlton never missed his daughter's birthday except the time he did jury service."

Spotting a fresh lead, Angel began to give out orders. "Right. You check, Raven. Was Edward Jackson ever sitting in court when Carlton Reed was a juror? Is there a link? Were the other victims ever jurors? Was it at the same time or even the same trial?" He paused to take a breath. "Jordan. Find out when Carlton Reed did his jury service. Okay?"

"Sure."

"And you're in contact with Paige Ottaway's family," he added, "so ask them as well. Just in case Raven can't find what we need in official databases."

"Done."

14 TROUBLING INFORMATION

In the workshop, Jordan watched Kate slotting an updated circuit board into the computer behind the Jag's dashboard. At the same time, he said into his phone, "Yes. Jordan Stryker. I dropped by on Tuesday and talked about Carlton."

"I remember," Demi replied. "And you say you've got another question?"

"Yes. You told me Carlton missed your daughter's birthday once because he was on a jury."

"True."

"When was that?"

"Well, it would've been January. The thirtieth. Which year? Let me see. 2008. Yes. 2008."

"Did he tell you the judge's name?"

"I don't think so."

"Or who was on trial and what for?"

"They told him not to discuss anything outside the courtroom."

"Yeah," Jordan said, walking round to the front of his car. "But did he?"

"Do juries swear on a bible or is that just the witnesses? Anyway, he was a God-fearing man who would've kept his word."

"Okay. Thanks. That's good."

"You're welcome. God bless."

Jordan paused. A technician had his head under the bonnet to install a new electronic starter unit. Its brand new microchips had come from a fresh source in Cardiff, so they were almost certainly untainted.

Redialling, Jordan called Sam Ottaway. "Hi," he said. "It's Jordan Stryker here. Just wondering if your dad's all right now."

"He's doing great," Sam replied. "He says thank you. I told him what you did. Oh. I asked him about forew as well. It didn't mean anything to him. Sorry."

"Shame," Jordan replied. "But I'm glad he's okay. Just one more thing. Do you know if your mum was ever on a jury?"

"No idea. What's it got to do with her accident?"

"I'm not sure. Maybe nothing. It's just something I'm working on."

"Well," Sam said, "it's the sort of thing she would've been happy to do. Serving the community and all that."

"It would've been early in 2008."

"Dad'll probably know. I'll ask him when I go to the hospital. All right? I'll call you back."

"Thanks," said Jordan.

The familiar and distinctive smell of Raven's perfume clung to the underground room. Normally restless, Raven sat motionless in front of her monitor. She said, "I've done all I can. I've accessed the jury database and our victims' names just don't crop up — not even Carlton Reed's. Are you sure his wife's got this right?"

Jordan shrugged. "She seemed to know what she was talking about."

"I cross-checked with Justice Jackson cases going back years. There's nothing."

"Not even in January 2008?"

"Not then, not anytime."

Jordan thought about it for a moment. "I can't see any reason why Demi Reed would lie or make it up, so why isn't Carlton's name on the database?"

"Short Circuit's pretty smart with a computer," Raven replied.

Jordan turned towards her. "Do you mean he could've got into it and deleted something or other?"

Raven took a deep breath. "He'd have to get past some heavy protection. I can get in because I've got high-level clearance. If Short Circuit hasn't, he'd have to be red hot to hack into these sorts of files. But I guess he is."

"Yeah."

"By the way," she said, "I've got that HiSpec list for you, whittled down to fifty-four people with the expertise and authority to influence chip design. I copied it into your part of the system."

He nodded. "Thanks. Still fifty-four, though?"

She frowned, apparently taking his comment as a criticism. "You should be pleased. That's a lot better than 613."

"I guess so. I'll take a look."

* * *

Jordan's relentless afternoon of phone calls continued. His mobile hardly left his hand. "Hello? Is that Jordan Stryker?"

"Yes."

"It's Dipak Hardikar. I've got some news for you."

Jordan looked around. Raven was not within hearing. "Great. What is it?"

"Not so great, I'm afraid. Madison Flint died in an accident sixteen months ago."

"What happened?"

"A woman's car broke down on an unmanned level crossing. A train ploughed into it. Big crash – and quite a lot of confusion. They thought five had died, but it turned out to be six. Madison Flint was one of them."

"Is there a description of her?"

"Better than that. A newspaper printed pictures of all the victims. Just their faces."

"Can you send Madison Flint's mugshot to my phone?"

"Not immediately. Let me ring off and I'll do it in a minute."

"Okay. Thanks."

Jordan ended the call but kept the mobile in his palm. Every few seconds, he glanced down at it, hoping to see Madison Flint, half knowing what to expect.

The phone bleeped when the image arrived. Even though he'd anticipated the face he would see, he still drew in a sharp breath. He recognized her immediately. Madison Flint was undoubtedly a slightly younger version of Raven.

But what did it mean? Why hadn't she told him that she once worked at HiSpec?

Raven probably deleted her real name from the list to cover up her past. That seemed to be the way in Unit Red. She had apparently died – like Ben Smith – and then resurfaced as an agent with an entirely different name – like Jordan Stryker. In reality, she probably hadn't been anywhere near that train crash. Angel was powerful enough to arrange a funeral for Ben Smith and alter the details of Phil Lazenby's death. He'd probably set up this fiction so Madison could disown her history and emerge as Raven.

But Jordan feared there was an alternative explanation. Raven had suggested that Short Circuit might be a microchip designer at HiSpec. Maybe she was right. But Raven herself had been a microchip designer at HiSpec. By removing her old name from the HiSpec staff list, was Raven hiding her past identity or the possibility that she was a murderer? And what was Jordan going to do about it?

Coming into the room, Angel interrupted Jordan's thoughts. "That amateur pilot who got on board Flight BA460 was quite like Toby Cotterill. But natural similarity wasn't enough. He'd had plastic surgery to finish the job. Anyway, I've checked him out. No particular knowledge of electronics and no connection with Suffolk. He's not Short Circuit. As far as I can see, you stumbled on a different plot altogether. I've given him to the normal security services."

"Okay," Jordan replied.

"Is something bothering you?"

"Er...no." Jordan wasn't yet ready to talk about Raven. First, he wanted to make up his mind how to deal with the troubling information he'd just received.

Angel frowned. "Sure?"

"Yes."

It wasn't true, of course. He felt utterly unsure.

Angel's sudden appearance reminded Jordan that, when he'd phoned from Ipswich, his chief had said, "I don't know where Raven is, but she's not here." That meant Raven too could have been in Ipswich. And, with her inside knowledge, she would know enough to take control of his Jaguar for one disastrous minute.

"All right," Angel said, realizing that Jordan didn't want a discussion. "I'll leave you to it. But first..." He handed Jordan a British passport. "That's for your hacker, Dipak Hardikar."

Straight after breakfast on Friday, Jordan took Kate into the cemetery where they would not be overheard. There, he told her that Madison Flint had been Raven's name before she'd joined Unit Red.

"Ah, that's it, then," Kate replied as they strolled past the overgrown monuments. "She was just covering up her history when she scrubbed that name from the HiSpec list. It's not a big deal."

"But..."

"What?"

"You know when we were in Sudbury? Where was Raven?"

Kate inclined her head in the direction of the Unit Red house. "Here. You called her on the way back to London."

"That was late. Where was she when Victoria Truman and the judge died?"

Kate came to a sudden stop. "What are you saying?"

Jordan shrugged. "I'm just...thinking aloud. She doesn't like me. Keeps giving me funny looks."

"Haven't you worked out why? I reckon she's wary of

you because she can never be sure she's private when you're around. Know what I mean?"

He nodded. She was referring to his terahertz vision. "But I haven't looked through her clothes. To be honest, there's not much to look at."

Relaxing, Kate laughed. "But she's proud of what she's got. A bit vain, even."

As they resumed their walk, Jordan gazed at his handler. "You don't seem so touchy about it."

"I'm a firefighter and engineer – or I was. Surrounded by big beefy blokes. I couldn't afford to be precious about such things. You ought to have heard the comments. On second thoughts, maybe you shouldn't." She hesitated before changing the subject. "Short Circuit didn't have to be in Sudbury, you know. If he's doing it all by hacking, he could be anywhere as long as he's in front of a computer."

"He's got to be close if he's using hardware Trojans. That's what Raven said. Either way, he – or she – must have been in Ipswich on Saturday to know Phil Lazenby was in my car."

"True," said Kate. "Good point."

Interrupted by the ringing of his phone, Jordan stopped by a crooked cross and answered the call.

"I've been on this all night," Dipak complained. "I'm

getting nowhere with HiSpec's bank and the workers on its payroll now."

"Forget it, then," Jordan replied. "Anything else?"

"You asked me about four people. Phil Lazenby, Carlton Reed, Paige Ottaway and Victoria Truman. I found out lots about the pilot, the bass player and the councillor, but Victoria Truman's a blank and there's nothing that links them all."

"Oh. That's a shame. To say the least."

"If I can't find it, I doubt if anyone can," Dipak said. "In fact, if I can't find it, I doubt if it exists."

Jordan sighed.

"I've done all I can," Dipak continued, "so what about my passport?"

"I've got it. I'll put it in the post today. And thanks."

Jordan ended the call. He was about to put his mobile back in his pocket when it rang again. This time, it was Sam Ottaway. Paige's son said, "Dad's not precise about when, but he reckons Mum did jury service quite a few years ago."

At once, Jordan's heart began to beat faster. "Is he sure? It's important."

"Is it?"

"Yes," Jordan said.

"Well, he's sure. He remembers because she was

proud of being made the jury foreman."

"Did she say what the case was?"

"I don't think so. Anyway," Sam said, "I don't see what it's got to do with Mum's treatment and the hospital's mistake."

"Neither do I," Jordan replied. "But there might be a connection. Thanks."

Straight away, he said to Kate, "Paige Ottaway was on jury service."

"It's beginning to look significant."

"Yes. She was foreman of the jury."

Kate smiled. "I think you'll find she was *forewoman*."

Jordan's mouth opened and he stared at her, his spine tingling.

"What have I said?" she asked.

"Forewoman. Which begins with forew. Which is as far as Phil Lazenby got when the car went into overdrive. I bet he was writing *forewoman* on her photo. He recognized her! He must have done. He must have been on the same jury!"

15 OPEN DISTRUST

"Right," Angel said. "Jordan's onto something. It looks like Phil Lazenby, Paige Ottaway and Carlton Reed were on jury service in East Anglia. And Justice Jackson was in the same area. You can link Lazenby to Ottaway for sure, because of what he wrote in the car, but I don't yet see a certain connection to the others."

"They're all dead," Jordan replied immediately.

"Through electronic mishaps," Kate added.

Angel nodded. "Mmm. But strangely, we haven't got

an official record of them being on the same jury – or any jury, if it comes to that. I suppose Short Circuit – clever with computers – could have hacked his way in there and destroyed the jury list." He looked around at them all. "So, what's our next move?" He was probably full of ideas, but he wanted to hear theirs.

Jordan was not going to announce his intentions when there was a chance that Short Circuit was in the room. He was concerned that Raven had the necessary clearance to open and perhaps alter the jury database. Knowing that she'd already deleted an entry from the HiSpec file, he was wondering if she had tinkered with the court records as well.

"Because," Angel continued, "it strikes me it's rather important. If we identified the trial – if they were all involved in the same one – we'd probably know who Short Circuit is. He'd be the one accused of a crime. Remember what he said in one of his rants? It's all about dignity and fairness. Maybe now we know what sort of grievance he's got. If he was on trial, he probably thinks it wasn't fair. That'd be his motive: revenge for his appearance in court. So, if we had a list of jurors, the prosecution barrister and the police officer in charge of the case, we'd probably know his next victims. In Short Circuit's eyes, they'd all be responsible for denting his dignity."

* * *

Jordan leaped up and, at full stretch, plucked a cricket ball from the air with his right hand. He threw it to the young bowler who, taken aback by the speed of the return, dropped the ball and blew on his stinging palms. At once, the boys began to argue among themselves. They were split on whether a player could be dismissed by a passing stranger taking a catch. Jordan smiled and continued to wander through Waterlow Park.

He was thinking about the latest theory. If Short Circuit had been on trial, surely he wouldn't have a motive for revenge unless he'd been found guilty of something. So, if he'd worked at HiSpec, one of the fifty-four employees with design experience would have a criminal record, dating from early 2008. That was what Jordan was keen to check.

Even if Short Circuit had been able to cover his tracks by deleting the jury list for a single trial, surely he couldn't have removed all trace of a criminal record. Jordan wasn't an expert, but he imagined that the police would keep details. The prison service would as well, if Short Circuit had been sent to jail. The conviction might have been reported in the press. Somewhere, there had to be a file containing the crime and the sentence. And, of course, the offender's name.

Raven would know where to look and she would have the clearance to access it. But could Jordan really trust her to do the research? He was caught in a dilemma. He wanted to check if Madison Flint had a criminal record, but he needed Raven's help to do so.

He sat down on a bench and, for a few seconds, closed his eyes. He took two deep breaths and then made up his mind. He would return to the house and confront her. He didn't have much choice. He wasn't looking forward to it, though.

In the computer room, Jordan looked at Raven and said, "Working on Short Circuit? What's your plan?"

She glanced at him briefly before turning back to her monitor. "I'll let you know if I get anywhere."

"If one of those HiSpec workers is Short Circuit," he said, "they could have a criminal conviction."

In a tone that suggested he'd insulted her intelligence, she replied with heavy sarcasm, "Really? I wish I'd thought of that."

Jordan steeled himself. "There's an obvious candidate, but she's not on the list."

Immediately, Raven spun on her chair and stared at him. "What do you mean?"

"I think you know what I mean. I'm talking about Madison Flint."

Raven swallowed and the muscles in her neck tensed. She glanced around the room as if checking that no one else was within hearing. "So, you've done some detective work behind the scenes."

He nodded. "You could say that."

"And you think I'm Short Circuit?"

"There's got to be a reason you didn't tell me you worked at HiSpec. I don't know what it is, though."

"I'm the one who put you onto HiSpec in the first place," Raven reminded him. "I'm hardly likely to do that if I'm Short Circuit, am I? That'd be pointing you in my direction."

Jordan's memory of that conversation was a little different. She'd certainly talked about HiSpec MicroSystems, but only after he and Kate had pushed her for the information. "So, why didn't you tell me you used to work there?"

"I didn't want you to get the wrong idea about me."

"Sure, but..."

Raven sighed. "Look. I was young. All right? I did some crazy things. I had to resign. I didn't exactly come clean about it. I hid it from Angel and Unit Red. That's all. It doesn't make me a murderer, you know. It makes me...a bit slippery. No more than that."

It was a straightforward matter of deciding whether she was telling the truth. Or had he heard another invention? "Why did you get kicked out of HiSpec?"

"Misusing computers," she replied. "Everyone did a bit of personal stuff on the side. Everyone looked at things that were nothing to do with work. I was the one they made an example of. And, before you ask, I didn't get hauled up in court for it." She pointed at her screen and added, "But I'd be interested if anyone else did."

"Are you getting anywhere?"

"A complete blank so far," she replied, "but I'm not halfway through the names yet."

"You must know them."

"I remember a few, yes, but only vaguely."

"Wouldn't you know if the cops had visited any of them?"

Raven grimaced. "I wouldn't be slaving over a hot computer if I did. I'd just tell you."

"Okay. Will you come and get me if you find anything?"

"Yes." She faced him once more and said, "Are you going to Angel?"

Jordan shook his head. "Why should I?"

"To tell him what you've just found out."

It hadn't occurred to Jordan. When he still went to a normal school, none of the students reported anything to the teachers. If there was a disagreement, the kids sorted it out between themselves, one way or another. "No," he said. "This is between you and me. Oh. I mentioned it to Kate, but no one else. I'll keep it that way unless..."

"Unless what?"

Jordan didn't really want to say it, but she was forcing him. "Unless things stack up against you, making you look like Short Circuit."

"So, you don't trust me one hundred per cent."

"How can I?"

Finally, Raven smiled. "I guess that evens us up. We're both cautious of each other."

"Me?" Jordan replied. "What have I done?"

"I don't know. That's the whole point. It's creepy that you can see more than I want to show – and I'd know nothing about it."

Kate was right that she disliked his terahertz vision. "So," Jordan said, "you don't trust me one hundred per cent either."

Raven's grin widened. "I think that's called a one-all draw."

Jordan left feeling pleased that he'd raised his

suspicions with her. He left feeling more relaxed about her. A relationship built on open distrust was at least an honest and workable relationship.

The loudspeakers in Jordan's bedroom belted out the Lemon Jelly song, the voice of the ramblin' man delivering the long list of places that he'd visited. Really, the catalogue of towns, cities and countries was so vast that it could have been a total coincidence that Short Circuit had struck in several of them. Jordan listened to it twice, convinced that he hadn't overlooked anything significant, convinced that the song and its bizarre lyrics were irrelevant.

He lay back on his bed and sighed.

Hearing a knock on the door, Jordan called out, "Hello?"

A heavily made-up face and a cascade of black hair appeared around the door. "Can I come in?" Raven asked.

"Sure." Jordan sat up straight, resting his back on the bedhead and pointed her towards the chair.

"We need to talk," she said, but she didn't sit down.

"Any luck with the list?"

She shook her head. "No luck involved. Just sheer hard work and talent."

He smiled at her. "What have you got?"

"According to the Prison Service, Eli Kennington was locked up in 2008 for hacking into sensitive government documents – MI5 and that sort of thing. He was a HiSpec designer and he served a couple of years for several violations of the Computer Misuse Act."

"Brilliant!" Jordan exclaimed, jumping up from his bed. "Have you told Angel?"

"Not yet. You want to ask me a question in private first."

"Do I?"

"Think about it."

Jordan nodded. "Yes. Did you know him?"

"Sort of. But he seemed so...innocent. Kept himself very much to himself. Autistic, I think. Or is it Asperger's syndrome? I'm not sure if there's a difference. Anyway, he didn't have any friends. No social skills at all. He had a reputation for being clumsy as far as I remember, but the company thought he was the bee's knees. I didn't even know he'd done a stretch in prison until five minutes ago. The story at the time was that he'd gone on an extended sabbatical." Seeing Jordan's puzzled expression, she added, "Basically, a long holiday. I guess it was the company's way of covering up for their favourite employee. They liked him so much they took him back afterwards.

That'd be because he hadn't harmed HiSpec at all."

"And that's when he started corrupting the design of their chips? After a stretch inside."

"I guess so," Raven said. "If we're right, he was preparing to get his own back on everyone who put him away. He honed his hacking skills or made a load of hardware Trojans."

Another head appeared round Jordan's door. This time, it was Kate, and she was plainly surprised to find Jordan and Raven together. "Oh," she said. "Sorry. Urgent meeting in the bunker. Another message has come in from Short Circuit."

"Okay," Angel said. "This is what's just arrived from Manchester Police. Don't get excited, though. I've listened to it and he's telling us – in his own peculiar way – what he thinks we've figured out already." He hit the return key of his computer and the familiar, highly distorted voice filled the room.

Friday 18th May: Justice Edward Jackson.

Immediately, there was a noise like a snort on the sound file.

There was not one drop of justice in him. I don't know why judges are called Justices. In court, they dispense the law, not justice. That's what I think. But I am getting ahead of myself. Everything has got to be in the right order. Here's the proper timeline.

Tuesday 31st January: Paige Ottaway had laser surgery on her brain. I'm pleased I found out about that. It all went wrong actually but the result was good.

Saturday 11th Feb: I don't care for music. Carlton Reed, the bass player, never made it home from Ecuador. My first downed flight. Easy.

Monday 5th March: Second downed flight. I'll give Captain Phil Lazenby credit for being a good pilot. He landed the plane and walked away from it. Actually, I'm not sure if it's right to talk about landing a plane when it splashed down in a river. Landing should mean coming down on land, I would have thought.

Friday 18th May: When I last met Victoria Truman, she was healthy. She made a mistake and got sick. I don't suppose one caused the other. Her disease was taking its time, though, so I hurried her along. And that brings me back to

Justice Edward Jackson. I know from experience that he's heartless. On Friday 18th May, I made sure he'd got no heart at all.

The next day – last Saturday – Captain Lazenby's credit finally ran out.

Sunday 27th May... Oh, I'm getting ahead of myself again. I can't mention what I haven't done yet. That would not be right. Sunday's the big one – when it all kicks off. I'm practised enough. I'm confident. I am ready to destroy society.

When the sound file ended, there was silence in the bunker until Angel said, "See what I mean? He's opened up because he reckons his motive's out of the bag. As soon as he killed a judge, he knew we'd start piecing together a trial and a jury."

Jordan said, "We know more than he thinks."

"Oh?" Angel prompted, gazing at Jordan.

"Raven? You did it, not me."

Raven seemed surprised that Jordan was giving her the opportunity to shine. "We've got a credible suspect," she announced, telling Angel and Kate everything she'd discovered from the Prison Service database.

"Right," Angel said. "Get on to it. Find out where he lives, Jordan. Pay him a visit. If he's not at home, maybe he's still working at HiSpec, so get in there. I don't care how you do it. If the company doesn't cooperate, use any means possible. We don't have time to be polite. You heard Short Circuit. He's going to do something big on Sunday. We haven't identified his likely targets, so we can't protect them. We've got to go after him instead. We've got tonight and tomorrow to find out if Eli Kennington really is Short Circuit. That's all." He looked at Kate and asked, "Is the Jaguar anything like ready?"

"Not a hundred per cent, but..."

"It'll have to do," said Angel. "You're back at the wheel, Jordan."

16 CAR CHASE

Some teenagers – almost certainly university students –
were talking loudly by the unlit lamp at the end of the
street. Darkness had not yet cloaked Cambridge, but the
students had probably enjoyed a few drinks already.
The rest of the road was quiet.

Jordan got out of his Jaguar and surveyed the front of
Eli Kennington's home. It was part of a terrace of narrow
houses. The small garden was overgrown and much of
the paint had flaked off the door and window frames.

The state of the place suggested the owner didn't have much time or money. Jordan imagined HiSpec would pay a valued designer very well, so Kennington was probably too busy to look after his home. Perhaps he was also too occupied to find himself a better house.

There was no answer to the doorbell. Jordan's fine hearing detected the faint chime from inside so he knew that it was working. He tried it again, but no one seemed to be home. The stakes were far too high to walk away, but Jordan felt too exposed to break into the house from the front, especially with an audience of students.

Making a mental note of the number of houses, he strode to the end of the street, round the corner and through the parking area by the River Cam. He doubled back along the alleyway behind the terrace and stopped when he'd counted back to Eli Kennington's property. The rear of the house seemed to be in slightly better condition than the front, but it certainly wasn't well maintained. Jordan sneaked up to the back door. It looked quite solid. The kitchen window frame was rotten, though. It didn't take much force from his right arm to split the wood and yank the window open. Wasting no time, he clambered inside.

He was standing in the sink, beside a draining board that was stacked with used bowls, mugs and glasses.

Jumping down, Jordan noticed that every surface of the kitchen – including the floor – was littered with plates, pots, pans and cutlery, both clean and dirty. Obviously, Eli Kennington had no time to look after his living space either.

Half of the hallway was piled high with junk that had probably been salvaged from skips around Cambridge. It left only a narrow gap for squeezing between rooms. The bathroom was not dirty, but every other room was obstructed by clutter. The living room was an amazing sight. It was filled with cannibalized computers, circuit boards, voltmeters, and other components. Jordan suspected that they'd been reclaimed from all sorts of discarded electrical equipment. Twisted wires dangled down from every shelf, chair and table. The entire room was a weird electronic grotto.

Surrounded by Eli Kennington's mess, Jordan had to remind himself that it wasn't a crime to be the ultimate geek and an obsessive collector. An unusual lifestyle didn't make Eli Kennington guilty of murder.

Hearing a car engine decelerate, Jordan ducked down and made his way to the window. Outside, a blue Nissan slowed down as it approached his Jaguar. Then it swerved round his parked car and sped to the residents' parking area. Tyres screeching, it executed a U-turn and suddenly accelerated back past the house. Jordan couldn't see the driver clearly, but it was a man.

Guessing that Eli had just returned but taken fright when he'd seen the Jag, Jordan dashed out of the front door, jumped into his car and took off after the Nissan. Following it, he turned right and headed north-east.

He wasn't close to the Nissan but his eyesight on maximum could pick out its registration. "Give me a trace on CE12 XTX. Does it belong to Eli Kennington?" Jordan barked into the hands-free secure phone.

"Searching," Raven's voice replied.

"What's happening?" Angel asked.

"A man was coming to Kennington's house but he took off instead."

Keeping his eye on the distant Nissan, Jordan put his foot down. There was little response. One of the most powerful cars on the planet was keeping to a steady thirty.

"Did he see you?" said Angel.

"No chance."

Raven interrupted. "Confirmed. It's Kennington's."

Angel continued, "Did he see the Jag?"

"Sorry. I didn't think," Jordan answered. "It was right outside his house."

Angel's voice became urgent. "Short Circuit would

recognize it from Ipswich when he used it as a weapon against Phil Lazenby. If Eli Kennington recognized it, that tells us who he is. Don't let him get away, Jordan."

Spinning the wheel to avoid three cyclists, Jordan said, "Tricky. No one told me how to override the speed limiter."

"Stay on air. I'll consult."

Ahead of him, two students were carrying a mattress across the urban road. A man at the front and a young woman at the back, they were holding it upright so it blocked Jordan's view. He knew only that Eli Kennington's car was speeding towards a traffic island. Jordan cursed under his breath. Closing in on the obstacle, his collision avoidance system began to slow the Jaguar automatically. The woman let her end of the heavy mattress slip from her grasp and it hit the tarmac. She giggled and said something to her companion. Jordan broke into a sweat. By way of an apology, she waved a hand at him. Then she clutched the mattress awkwardly and manoeuvred it out of his way.

Luckily, the road in front of him was straight and Jordan caught sight of the Nissan turning left at a large roundabout.

Angel's voice boomed into the car. "Right. It's quick and easy. Think your way through the on-board computer to *Speed Limiter*. Your password is like an on/off switch. Enter it and you're away."

The Jag responded immediately. Its rapid acceleration pushed Jordan against the backrest of the driver's seat. He zoomed up to the wooded traffic island and swung to the left. But he'd lost sight of Kennington.

There was another roundabout ahead. The third exit was Milton Road, a major route out of Cambridge. Guessing that Kennington might have taken that turn, Jordan tried it as well.

Two hundred metres ahead, there was a set of traffic lights on red. As he neared the junction, the lights turned green. Pulling out of the lane as much as the oncoming traffic allowed, Jordan spotted the Nissan at the head of the queue. Breathing a sigh of relief, he said aloud, "I'm still behind him. On the A1309, north out of Cambridge."

"We're tracking your GPS signal here," Angel told him. "I don't have backup in the area, so it's up to you."

"The signs say the A14's just up here."

"He'd be a fool to go on that. He'll never outrun you on a dual carriageway. The Jag's too powerful."

"Maybe he doesn't know I'm behind him," Jordan replied.

"Thinking about it, maybe he does and he wants you on a fast road. If he's Short Circuit, he's controlled the Jag before. Maybe he's expecting to do it again. He wants you tearing down the road so he can make you swerve and cause an accident."

Jordan swallowed. "Are you sure he can't?"

"All the car's main controlling systems are new. He might be able to flash your lights, start your wipers or whatever, but nothing important."

Raven's voice broke into the conversation. "You're safe. What can he do to you while he's driving?"

Going past the entrance to the Science Park, Jordan peered ahead and said, "He's pulled over to the right." Jordan eased into the same lane, three cars behind him, and followed him around the giant traffic island. "Yes," Jordan announced, "it's the A14 east."

"Good," Angel replied. "You can catch him whenever you want."

"Then what?" Jordan asked.

"Let's see what develops. First, get behind him. Not too close, though. Don't make yourself too obvious."

Checking his mirror, Jordan joined the main carriageway and accelerated. As he closed in on the Nissan, he was well aware that there were several microprocessors inside him that Short Circuit could probably disrupt. But, even if Eli Kennington was Short Circuit, he couldn't possibly know that Jordan was enhanced. Until they stopped driving and came face-to-face, Jordan had no reason to fear an electronic assault on his body.

Was he really so close to Short Circuit? Was that who he was chasing along the A14 towards Bury? When Kennington had seen the Jag outside his house, he'd taken off at speed and that made him look guilty. But Jordan wasn't convinced by a mere impression. After all, Dipak Hardikar had also tried to get away from him, when he'd left WT Gaming and Programming in a panic, but it wasn't because Dipak was Short Circuit. Perhaps there was some other reason why Eli Kennington had fled. Having once been investigated, convicted and imprisoned, maybe he was simply nervous.

Overtaking a lorry effortlessly, Jordan could see that there was only one car separating him from the blue Nissan. He didn't want to make it plain that he was tailing Kennington. Deciding he was close enough, he eased off the accelerator and matched the Nissan's speed.

After only five kilometres, Kennington swung his car on to a slip road at the last moment. Jordan barely had time to report the unexpected lurch to the left before doing the same himself. "Taking next junction. A1303."

The slip road led to another large traffic island. The Nissan hardly slowed at the give way sign but Jordan had to wait for three cars. "Left goes to Newmarket," he told Angel and Raven. "Right goes back to Cambridge. That's the one he's taken."

There was a moment's pause before Angel's voice said, "Probably means he's rumbled you. He's playing games. Maybe trying to throw you off his scent. I bet he takes a few turns as soon as he's out of your sight."

Jordan took off across the roundabout, streaked round the bends and onto the Cambridge road. As soon as it straightened, he let out a groan. There was no sign of the Nissan ahead. "You're right," Jordan said as he pulled onto the verge. "He's gone."

He opened the driver's window and listened carefully. He could hear the constant drone of speeding cars on the main road but, as well as that, he could just make out an idling engine nearby. He got out of the Jaguar and turned his neck from side to side, pinpointing the sound. It was somewhere in front of him and to the left.

Walking down the road, the rumbling grew louder in his enhanced hearing. Smiling now, he moved towards a gap in the hedgerow. It was a dirt track leading into flat farmland. As soon as he ventured into the field, an engine roared on his right. Kennington had hidden his car behind the high hedge. Before Jordan could dive out of the way, Kennington accelerated. The bumper took his legs from under him and scooped him up. The car spun back towards the road and Jordan rolled off the bonnet. He landed with a heavy thud on the damp earth.

The Nissan didn't speed away immediately. Eli Kennington opened his window and looked back. With an expression of surprise and intrigue on his face, he gazed in particular at the robotic fingers of Jordan's right hand which were twitching unnaturally. Then, without a word, he put his foot down and returned to the A14 roundabout.

Jordan regained control over his arm, but the pain in both of his legs stopped him getting to his feet immediately and rushing to the XJ. He managed only to stagger to the edge of the road and watch Eli Kennington drive straight on at the traffic island, away from Cambridge and towards Newmarket.

17 TOTALLY FURIOUS

"If he's Short Circuit," Jordan said into his phone, as he limped across the electronic cavern that was Eli Kennington's living room, "there's going to be a note here somewhere — maybe on a computer — of everyone who put him in prison. I'm after his hit list."

"And it's important to get it if it's there," Kate replied, "but, first, what if he comes back?"

"I've scared him off for now. He went in the opposite direction," said Jordan.

"All right. But are you okay?"

"Sure. I don't think I'd be walking – well, hobbling around – if I'd broken something. I'm just bruised."

There was a delay before Kate replied, "Angel wants to talk to you."

Jordan waited.

Then Angel's voice sounded in his ear. "Have you parked your car right outside again?"

"No. It's round the corner, out of sight."

"I don't think it'll be long before he heads for home," said Angel. "I've been looking into his records. Very illuminating."

"Like?"

"I haven't got anything up-to-date. He hasn't been to see a doctor in ages, but his medical history is fascinating. He's got Asperger's syndrome. Quite severe, in a way." Angel took a breath. "In a nutshell, he's highly intelligent, socially inept and unaware of other people's feelings. He has great difficulty in sleeping and he pursues narrow interests single-mindedly – to the exclusion of everything else. It's not a great surprise that his main enjoyment is computers and electronic gadgets."

Jordan leaned against the table to ease his aching legs.

"His psychologist's assessments and recordings are

enlightening as well." Angel was clearly reading as he continued, "He doesn't seek, initiate or develop friendships or share his interests or achievements because of failed social encounters in childhood."

Jordan interrupted. "That's sad."

"It fits with Short Circuit's threat to target everyone as well. Kennington doesn't engage with society so he'd be happy to destroy it. His mother said he used to scream until he went purple when he was a baby. She'd never seen such rage. There are some recordings of him when he was nine. I was so struck by this one, I remember every word. 'When I get stressed comes the anger. You have to understand, Asperger's amplifies any emotion, making it ten times better or worse. Happy Asperger's children laugh all the time. With me, it's anger. I go well past angry. I get totally furious. It consumes me. All I can see is darkness, and when it's gone, I've wrecked something.' And, yes, that came from the lips of a nine-year-old."

Jordan could still picture Kennington's innocent-looking face, gazing at him as he lay hurt on the farm track. There was no sympathy in his expression. There was only curiosity. Jordan asked Angel, "So, what makes you think he's on his way back here?"

"Where else would he go? He's a creature of habit,

Jordan. He can't cope with change. He'll return and he'll be upset – very upset."

"You mean he'll be angry."

"He could be totally furious."

"Are you saying I've got to get out?"

"Yes and no." Angel explained, "It's dangerous, but we need his hit list if he's got one."

"If he's Short Circuit," Jordan stressed.

"There's not much doubt about that now. But unfortunately you could be wasting your time. He might not have a written list at all. He's an obsessive. People like that amass information in their heads."

Jordan was surprised by the idea. "That's a lot of stuff he'd have to remember. Like Paige Ottaway's illness, when she was going into hospital, which hospital, what her operation was going to be and that sort of thing. Then there's Phil Lazenby's flights and the award ceremony. And that's just two of them. He'd have to memorize the names and details of everyone who put him away."

"I hope I'm wrong," Angel answered. "I hope there's a computer document or an old-fashioned notebook. That's the evidence we need. And it might tell us what he's targeting on Sunday. So, give yourself a limit – like quarter of an hour. Then get out. And keep your hearing on maximum while you search."

"Okay."

But it turned out to be longer than quarter of an hour. The living room alone was so messy that it would take hours to sift thoroughly. Jordan unearthed a working computer, but he couldn't get past a password that protected all of the stored documents. The icons that littered the screen were almost all unfamiliar to Jordan. They activated programs he'd never seen before and he didn't know what they did.

On a long shelf, Jordan recognized a butchered PlayStation, several mobile phones, two SatNav devices, an iPod and a DVD player. They lay around like patients with open wounds and their innards showing. There were memory sticks and computer CDs everywhere Jordan looked. Any of them could contain vital information. Really, he needed a specialized team to help him search for evidence.

There was less paperwork to browse. The sheets that he did find were puzzling. There were pieces torn from newspapers, a manual that bore the HiSpec MicroSystems logo and a few scraps of incomprehensible notes in untidy handwriting. Nothing seemed to relate to Short Circuit's activities.

Jordan stood in the middle of the electronic jungle and wondered if he'd tangled with a very odd but harmless character. He wasn't even certain that Kennington had meant to knock him down on the dirt track. The face that had peered out at him from the driver's window belonged to a man of about thirty years of age, with stubble from his mouth to his ears, yet there was something about his expression that was naïve, almost endearing. Maybe it was because he had the bright, pure eyes of a baby.

Jordan's robotic arm felt heavy. It twitched twice, reminding him of when it was first fitted, before he had it under control. He guessed that the random movement was down to his mind wandering or an electronic glitch.

Jordan was overwhelmed by the size of his task. He needed more time and help. He didn't want to leave without a clear sign of Kennington's innocence or guilt. But he also knew he should have left by now.

He looked back at the computer. Next to it was a printer/scanner that was stained with coffee. Jordan reached out for the paper tray, but he misjudged the distance and direction. His right arm clunked instead against the side of the machine. Suddenly he wasn't seeing properly. His eyesight ran through its bewildering wavelengths, making him dizzy. The edges of his vision collapsed to a red blur. He seemed to be looking at the printer through a glowing crimson tube.

Then his right arm fell uselessly to his side.

Knowing that the fault could be an electronic attack, he turned round frantically and looked out of the windows. Everything seemed to be getting darker as if a heavy storm cloud had gathered over Cambridge. Turning on the lights would not make a difference, though. The gloom was in his visual system. His audible range was also dwindling alarmingly. His ears could have been plugged with cotton wool.

The high-tech apparatus that made his life bearable seemed to be in terminal decline. He felt like a candle flame, flickering unsteadily as it consumed its final supply of wax. He slumped into a chair.

Jordan barely noticed Eli Kennington entering the room. His eyesight had weakened alarmingly. It was as bad as it had been straight after the explosion that had mangled his body. Eli was a fuzzy figure standing by the door, looking at him inquisitively. In one hand he carried a laptop, in the other a baseball bat.

"This is more than I hoped for," Eli said, coming forward with a bouncy walk. "At first, I thought you were a normal human being, but I saw this from the car." He put down the laptop, reached out and touched Jordan's artificial hand. "Now I see your whole arm is artificial. And there's more. You are nothing like normal. My hardware Trojans have done much more than put one limb out of action."

With his damaged hearing, Jordan had to concentrate to pick up Kennington's rapid-fire speech. Luckily, his voice was unusually loud.

"Your car is special as well," Eli continued. "I have disabled it."

"You can't have."

"I am not stupid. Parking it two streets away is not adequate protection."

"But you can't get into the new circuit boards."

Eli shook his head. "When I need creativity comes creativity. I let the tyres down."

Kennington wasn't furious. He might have been seething inside, but his curiosity was probably keeping a black mood at bay. Still wielding the baseball bat as a weapon, he grabbed a pair of ultra-sharp scissors and slipped one blade between Jordan's right wrist and his clothes. Then, in one swift movement, he sliced the sleeve up to the elbow. The material flopped open to reveal Jordan's flawless and hairless forearm.

Eli nodded. "That is very nice. I am looking forward to seeing the technology behind it. Is it controlled by your mind, with help from smart circuitry?"

"Yes."

"I want it," Eli said bluntly, like a toddler who had just seen a fantastic toy. "I am going to dismantle it, but not here."

Jordan had heard enough. He still wasn't sure whether this childlike grown-up was a murderer, but he wanted to escape or at least to regain control. Yet there was still that weighty baseball bat swaying in front of his hazy eyes. Kennington jiggled it around constantly in his hand.

Jordan waited, hoping for an opportunity, hoping that Eli would drop his guard for a moment. Without a functioning right arm, though, Jordan wasn't going to win a fight. His best chance, he thought, was simply to run. As long as he was first out of the front door, he thought he could get away. If he failed, Kennington would probably treat him like a piece of equipment he could strip of its valuable components.

"It was you controlling my car in Ipswich, wasn't it?"

"No."

Jordan was taken aback by the denial for an instant, but maybe Eli was acting like a child who refused to admit guilt even after being caught red-handed. "You're lying."

Eli looked offended. "I do not lie. I do not understand lies."

"You went to prison once, didn't you?" Jordan asked. "Why?"

For the first time, Kennington stopped moving around. He stared at the carpet for several seconds before answering. "The charge related to hacking. I found ways into government documents and MI5. They told me it was wrong. But it wasn't. I am not a terrorist or anything bad. I was doing it for fun. When there is challenge comes fun. I should never have been jailed."

"It sounds rough on you."

He lowered his eyes for a moment. "It was worse than rough."

Jordan could tell from his manner that he'd had a terrible time behind bars. He probably didn't have the temperament to thrive among prisoners. "You must hate the judge and jury who put you there."

"Yes." Simmering, he looked down at the baseball bat in his hand.

Jordan hadn't got proof that he'd found Short Circuit. Eli Kennington hadn't admitted anything. But he did look distracted by thoughts of prison and that was Jordan's cue. He jumped up as quickly as his disabled body would allow and made a dash to the door. But he was too clumsy and lopsided. Eli's temper erupted before he could escape. Jordan felt a crack on his head and he lost consciousness.

18 THE SINGULARITY

When Jordan woke, he found himself in the passenger's seat of a moving car. It was Eli Kennington's Nissan. He wasn't just pinned to the seat with the safety belt. Strong plastic ties encircled his body tightly. His view of the outside world was limited by his impaired vision and the extent of the headlights. The road was narrow and the countryside was utterly flat. They were probably driving through the farmlands of East Anglia.

Still groggy, Jordan asked, "Where are we going?"

"We are nearly there."

"Where?"

"We are going to my weekend hideout," Eli told him.

Jordan's head ached and his mouth was dry. Slowly, though, he was regaining his senses. He decided that the best plan was to keep calm and take no risks. At least, not until he felt up to it.

"I like getting away at weekends," Kennington continued. "I like getting away from people. Mostly, people like to see the back of me."

"But you're taking me with you," Jordan pointed out.

The car's headlights picked out a dark creature scurrying across the road in front of them. Jordan couldn't identify it.

"I am a loner," Eli said. "So are you. You're singular. I should think you are unique."

"Singular?"

Eli stared ahead. Not once had he made eye contact with Jordan. "You are between human and the singularity."

"The what?"

"That is the time when people merge with machines." He changed down a gear to take a sharp bend in the road. "I took a look at you before dragging you into the car. You have cameras in your eyes, at least two brain implants and maybe more things. You are part of the way to the singularity. You are privileged. When a human being and a machine become a single thing, the hybrid will be really smart and live for ever." He sounded gleeful at the prospect. "Now, I am privileged as well because I have found an early hybrid. I hope I didn't damage your brain implants when I got angry and hit you. I want them in working condition."

Jordan gulped. It sounded as if Kennington was planning to remove them. Jordan dreaded to think how he might do that.

Eli's hands made repetitive and unnecessary shuffling movements on the steering wheel as he drove. To the right, there were a few unfocused lights. Probably a village. Eli didn't take a right turn, though. He continued for a few minutes and then took a rough track on the left. The only lamps were dotted infrequently along the road behind them. Apart from the car's own headlights, it was pitch black in front.

Jordan tried to log on to the Unit Red system, but his brain/computer interface was not responding. There seemed to be a black hole in his pounding head. Fearing the worst, he asked, "Have you destroyed my microprocessors?"

"I have no reason to destroy the things I most admire.

I need to find out what they can do. They are no good to me if they are broken."

"So, what have you done to them?"

"They are in sleep mode. I can reactivate them any time – with my laptop." Kennington jerked his head towards the computer on the back seat. "I left your mobile in Cambridge. I don't want anyone using it to trace where I'm going. I am still wondering if you have an internal GPS system. If I turn you back on, you might start broadcasting my position. I need to check that first. I like to get away from people. I do not want them to find me."

Eli was speaking to Jordan but he was strangely detached. He hadn't even asked Jordan's name. And he didn't seem to be curious about who might be monitoring Jordan's location and why Jordan was pursuing him in the first place. Maybe he was so engrossed with the hijacking of Jordan's technology that he hadn't even thought of asking. Maybe it was simply irrelevant to him.

He stopped the car and announced, "We have arrived."

Jordan narrowed his eyes. Outside, he could just make out something tall and round, like a wide chimney, but nothing else. "What is it?" he asked.

"It used to be a windmill," Eli replied, "but it lost its

sails many years ago. I will take you in now." His loud voice seemed entirely inappropriate in the silence of the night.

"It's late."

Eli shrugged. "I do not sleep much."

"Do you eat?"

Eli looked puzzled. "Of course I eat. If I did not eat, I'd die. I'm not dead. I am alive."

"I was hinting."

"What are you hinting at?"

"I'm hungry. And thirsty."

"It is better to say what you mean. I do not do hints." Eli got out of the car, opened the back door and grasped his laptop and a plastic bag. "Come in nicely and I will give you some food." He held up the bag and added, "I stopped on the way and bought sandwiches, chocolate and a drink." Eli walked round the Nissan, opened the passenger door and unfastened Jordan's seat belt.

His arms held against his body by the plastic ties, Jordan wriggled awkwardly out of the car and stumbled towards the converted windmill. If his infrared vision had been working, the darkness would not have troubled him, but he could see very little. He knew he was in great danger, but he was not yet ready to try and escape because he still wanted answers from Eli Kennington. He was squirming like a hooked fish, willing to be played, but determined not to be reeled in completely.

Eli unlocked the door, stepped into the cottage and turned on the wall lights. Inside, there was just one perfectly circular room, split into sections. Half was a living space, a quarter was the kitchen and another quarter was the dining area. On the far side, a door led to a bathroom that had been added onto the basic structure of the windmill. A tight spiral staircase led to the bedroom area. Looking up, Jordan saw an old and thick oak beam that ran across the diameter of the building. Smaller beams sprouted upwards from it and supported the conical wooden roof. Two bright spotlights attached to the main beam cast more light into the ground floor.

Behind him, Eli locked the door from the inside and then slipped the key into his trouser pocket.

Perhaps the holiday cottage was a little tidier than Eli's home in Cambridge, but not a lot. Equipment was scattered everywhere. It looked like a computer company's scrapyard.

Eli removed some used plates from the dining table and put the bag of food in the middle. "I am eager to explore," he said, glancing at Jordan's arm, "but we will eat first."

"How?"

Kennington hesitated, not sure what Jordan meant for a moment. "Ah, yes. When you are tied up, you cannot put food in your mouth."

Jordan replied with a smile, "You could feed me."

"I'm not going to do that!" Eli almost shouted. "It is not dignified."

"I didn't mean it," said Jordan. "I was joking."

Eli was clearly bemused. "If you don't mean something, I suggest you do not say it. It is confusing otherwise. Now," he continued, "I am going to cut the ties so you can eat on your own, but I don't want you to run away with all those devices."

"I won't. I can't. You locked the door."

While Eli cut the plastic bands around his arms and stomach, Jordan said, "Don't you think at some point I'm going to put up a fight?"

Surprised by the idea, Kennington simply shook his head.

Taking the unexciting sandwich in his left hand, Jordan tried questioning the fidgety genius again. "Do you know Madison Flint?"

"No."

Jordan thought he answered too quickly. He didn't mean that he didn't know her. His rapid response suggested that he wasn't interested in thinking and then answering the question.

Jordan had another go. "She used to work at HiSpec. Madison Flint. Do you remember her? Long black hair."

This time, Eli stopped eating and took a deep breath. "Yes. Yes, I do. She..." He frowned as he tried to find the right words. "She wanted to be my friend."

"Oh? Did it work out?"

"What do you mean?"

"Did you become friends?" Jordan asked.

Not looking up at Jordan, he shook his head. "Not really, no. I think friends do more together than we ever did."

"What went wrong?"

Kennington shrugged. "I don't know. A relationship did not happen."

For a moment, Eli's reply sent Jordan's mind down a different course. If Raven felt sympathy for Kennington, she might feel angry that he'd been punished unjustly. She might strike at the system that had imprisoned him. There again, she'd told Jordan that she didn't know Eli Kennington had been jailed. She couldn't feel sorry for him when, at the time, she'd thought he was on holiday.

Jordan changed the subject. "Do you like music?"

Eli smiled to himself. "I don't understand it, but I like rhythm. I find it soothing."

His answer wasn't what Jordan was expecting. In his latest message, Short Circuit mentioned a dislike of music. "I'm a drummer," Jordan said. "A keeper of rhythm. Or at least, I was."

Kennington kept his eyes on his food or on Jordan's right arm. "They didn't have any cans. I bought a big bottle of drink. I'm not supposed to have fizzy, but that is what I got."

"Thanks."

He took the bottle to the kitchen work surface and, with his back to Jordan, poured the cola into two identical glasses. He loped back to the table, slopping one of the drinks slightly, and put both of the glasses down. Clearly not satisfied, he switched them round, pushing one towards Jordan.

At first, Jordan thought he was simply jiggling them round because he was restless and clumsy. But then he wondered if there was a different reason.

Jordan glanced around the cottage again. There were two narrow windows downstairs, one over the kitchen sink and another in the living space. He wasn't sure about the upstairs. He could just make out one small slot in the brickwork. Pointing to the door behind Eli, he asked, "What's that?"

Kennington twisted round in his seat. "A door."

"What's behind it?"

"It is a shower and toilet. Because of the round thin structure, it could not be fitted upstairs."

Jordan nodded and took a long drink of the cola. It wasn't cold, but it was refreshing.

Eli swigged his own back and, for the first time, glanced at Jordan's face. He put the empty tumbler down and said, "It is almost time I started."

Jordan knew exactly what Kennington meant. Fearing for his enhancements, he shivered. With his arm and brain implants still inoperative, he wasn't sure how to make his escape. But he had to do something and he had to do it soon.

"Do you really want to take me apart?" said Jordan. "You'd hold up the singularity for years. I'm a guinea pig for bionic bits and pieces."

Eli's face crinkled with confusion. "You are not a guinea pig."

"No, I mean, my body's used to test enhancements. I don't think you want to get in the way of progress, do you?"

"Certainly not, but..."

"But what?"

"The opportunity is impossible to resist. I want your components, not you."

"I'll help you take a look – to satisfy your curiosity – if you let me go afterwards."

Kennington shook his head. "I cannot let you stay whole because you would be able to choose what to do and what not to do. Your parts don't have a choice. Once I have worked them out, they will do what I want them to do."

"That's crazy," Jordan blurted out before he could stop himself.

"I am not mentally deficient or disabled. I just think differently. I think accurately. I give attention to detail." Gazing enthusiastically at Jordan's arm, he asked, "Does the skin unpeel?"

"Yes," Jordan answered. "But we'd need a technician to do it."

"I have a scalpel somewhere. That will suffice." He got up and began to search for it.

The chaos of the windmill gave Jordan time to think. He weighed up the evidence. Kennington had admitted that he hated the people who had put him away. He'd admitted that he'd made and triggered the hardware Trojans that had neutralized Jordan's enhancements.

And he'd kidnapped Jordan. He had the motive and the means to do everything that Short Circuit had done. The conclusion was obvious: Kennington was Short Circuit. But was that too easy?

Jordan tried to remember Short Circuit's messages, wondering if there was anything in them that would help him decide what to believe. *When it all kicks off*. That's what Short Circuit had said near the end of his last recording. Jordan was not convinced that Eli would come up with something like that. He spoke literally. He'd associate a kick-off only with football. For the same reason, Jordan also doubted that he'd refer to Captain Lazenby's credit having finally run out. When Short Circuit talked about Carlton Reed, he said that he didn't care for music, yet Eli found it soothing.

No matter how guilty Eli Kennington appeared, there was a chance he wasn't Short Circuit after all.

Glancing round the circular room, Jordan realized that Eli didn't have a television. There wasn't one in his Cambridge house either. "Do you like films and TV?"

Bent over the clutter on the couch, Eli answered without interrupting his hunt, "I don't understand what they are for."

So, Jordan asked himself, why did Short Circuit say

that films were very helpful in his message following the Quito disaster?

Eli stood upright with a small sharp scalpel in his hand. He smiled and advanced towards Jordan.

19 TOP PRIORITY

"Do you really expect me to just sit here and let you... do what you're going to do?"

Standing next to him with the blade in his hand, Kennington said, "I know you will." Then he yawned, drew up a chair and sat down wearily. Surprised by sudden exhaustion, he muttered, "I am tired."

"It's late," Jordan replied, wondering if he knew what was behind Eli's unexpected fatigue.

"But I do not get tired."

"What are you going to do on Sunday?"

Eli looked at the thin sharp blade in his hand. "I am dedicating the whole weekend to exploring your arm and head."

"Apart from that?"

"When I get interested in something, nothing else matters." His eyelids drooping, he looked oddly at Jordan and said, "Did you do anything to the drinks?"

"Yes," Jordan admitted. "I got you to turn your back for a few seconds and switched them round."

"So I drank yours!"

"Yes."

"Why did you do that?" Eli asked.

"Because you seemed nervous about who got which drink. You wanted me to have a particular one. I thought it'd be interesting to see what happened if you drank it instead."

"But..."

"Did you put something in it?"

Eli yawned again and struggled to keep his eyes open. "I take a lot of medication. I am an expert in pills. I have one that makes people very drowsy and it lowers their resistance. That is what I gave you."

Jordan smiled. "Sorry, but I didn't take it. You did. I'm not the one feeling dead beat."

Eli flopped in the chair.

Jordan seized the opportunity. He grabbed the scalpel and threw it awkwardly across the room with his left arm. When he stood up, Eli didn't react. He remained sprawled in his seat. His eyelids had closed.

Jordan leaned close and said, "You haven't murdered anyone, have you?"

Eli's eyes flickered open for a moment. "Murdering is not nice. It would not be a good thing to do."

Jordan delved into his trouser pocket and extracted the key. Squinting, he crossed the room, grabbed Eli's laptop and made for the front door. There was no challenge from Kennington. He seemed to be asleep. Jordan unlocked the door and left. Before making his getaway, though, he locked Kennington in his own holiday cottage.

Jordan decided not to take Eli's car. With little eyesight and only one ungainly arm, he doubted that he could drive safely. Instead, he walked back down the track, towards the main road and the village that he'd seen earlier.

Well beyond midnight, it was a clear and quiet night, but the cold wind blowing across the fields made Jordan shiver. He seemed to be the only person awake. No ghostly lights moved along the tarmac that divided the farmland. As he walked, he thought more about Eli

Kennington. If he was simply a strange and innocent man, who was guilty? Who was Short Circuit? Jordan's mind turned again towards his fellow agent. But he wasn't convinced. Even though Raven had tried to befriend Eli Kennington, she could not be acting out of sympathy for him because she hadn't known about his conviction. She had no reason to target everyone responsible for jailing him. It just didn't add up.

Maybe someone else involved in the court case was out for vengeance on Eli's behalf. Jordan didn't know a lot about trials, but there could have been a solitary juror who thought Kennington was innocent, but who'd been outvoted. Perhaps one of the officials who had defended Eli was now taking the law into his or her own hands.

Jordan froze. There was a faint rustling noise to his right. Someone or something was moving by the hedge. He could no longer pinpoint sounds, but he realized that the noise was coming from low down in the verge. He took a breath and moved on. He'd probably disturbed a bird or a rat.

He reached the village after an hour of brisk walking. But it was as quiet as a graveyard. With relief, though, he noticed that the pub was still lit. The main door was shut and refused to open. He could not even force his way in with his bionic arm. It still hung limply, like a

dead weight attached to his shoulder. Instead he knocked on the wooden door panels with his left fist. Getting no answer, he banged again and again. He refused to give up. After a few minutes, someone arrived on the other side and grumbled, "All right, all right! Do you know what time it is? We're closed." It was a woman's voice.

"There's been an accident," Jordan shouted back. "I'm hurt. I need help."

There was the sound of a bolt being withdrawn and a key turning, then the big door swung open. The woman was middle-aged, dressed in jeans and a blouse. She looked him up and down. "What's happened?"

Jordan pointed to his right arm. "I can't move it. It's broken. And my eyes are blurry. I can hardly see."

"You'd better come in and sit down," she said, standing to one side.

"Thanks. I just need to make a phone call really. I know someone who'll get me home."

She was still suspicious of him, but she said, "All right."

Even with a damaged sense of smell, Jordan recognized the beery aroma of a pub recently emptied of its customers. He stepped inside unsteadily and asked, "Where am I? What's this place called?"

* * *

Angel sent an engineer to Cambridge to retrieve Jordan's stranded Jaguar and his phone. He also sent a taxi to bring Jordan back to Highgate Village.

In the bunker, Jordan reported everything that had happened. He also handed Eli's laptop to Raven. "Kennington said he could reactivate all my microchips with that. Maybe you can instead."

At once, Angel said, "Get on to it, Raven. Top priority."

"All right," she replied. "But..."

"What?"

"It's tricky. I might be out of my depth."

Angel frowned. "I've never heard you say that before. I'll get our computer technicians in to help. That'll speed it up."

"Okay." Looking at Jordan, Raven added, "Before I check it out, just tell me. Was it Short Circuit you locked up in his own windmill?"

Jordan took a deep breath and then shook his head. "I don't think so."

Angel, Raven and Kate all looked astonished. "But he's a dead cert," said Raven.

Kate exclaimed, "He was going to pull you apart."

"Yeah, but that's just how he is. I don't think he'd murder anyone."

"He ran you over," said Raven.

"Maybe he didn't mean to. Maybe I was just in the way. I don't know. But, for some reason, I like him. He wasn't...complicated. He just said what he meant. And some of the things he said were the exact opposite of Short Circuit's messages."

"We need to know who else was involved in his trial," Angel decided. "Give me the key to his cottage and I'll send an agent to interrogate him. Maybe he can remember – if he's not Short Circuit himself."

Raven was so fixed on the laptop that she didn't notice Jordan coming into the underground computer room. She let out a cry and jumped when he asked, "How's it going?"

"You gave me a fright," she replied. "It's okay. Not brilliant, but okay. I've located a program called 'UnTrojan'. That's bound to be what we want, but I'm not sure how it works. The technicians will be able to help. They're due any second. I'll figure it out with them. You can't rush this. If you press the wrong button, it might demolish your control systems completely."

Jordan nodded. "Eli remembered you."

"Yeah? Well, I tried to engage with him – I tried to be kind – but you can't. Not with someone who's only interested in himself and gadgets." She paused before adding, "He's a good candidate for Short Circuit."

"Maybe, but..."

Raven interrupted. "You're inexperienced. Angel's sending a specialist to talk to him. Then we'll know." She looked into Jordan's face and added, "Go and get some rest. I don't need you yet. I'll come and get you when we're ready to kick-start your bits."

Jordan sighed. "All right. Thanks. I'm knackered."

Someone had got him by his arm. He could feel the fingers gripping his left elbow. He could feel the shaking. The movement dragged him back from sleep to wakefulness. "What...?"

Kate Stelfox was tugging at him and whispering into his ear. "Jordan! What you said got me wondering."

He groaned and opened his still feeble eyes. "What did I say?"

"About Raven," she said in a loud whisper. "I didn't think for a minute that she... But I made a few discreet enquiries and looked a few things up."

"What are you talking about?"

"I'm talking about where Raven was on the eleventh of February."

Finally Jordan shook off the numbness of sleep. "That's when the plane came down in Ecuador."

Kate nodded. "She was on a skiing holiday in Switzerland."

Jordan sat up in his bed. "Geography's not my strong point, but I don't think Switzerland's on the way to Ecuador."

"But I don't know for sure that she stayed in Switzerland the whole time. She went by train. They're the only records I could find. She could've flown on from Switzerland."

After his encounter with Eli Kennington, Jordan suspected that Short Circuit was using the same Trojan technology. Even so, he said, "I suppose a hacker could have crashed it from anywhere...even Australia."

"I haven't finished yet. It's quite a coincidence she was taking a long weekend when the Edinburgh crash happened. I don't know about the rest, but a while ago she arranged to have tomorrow off as well – exactly when Short Circuit's up to something. Angel says it's her job to help unlock your enhancements. If she does that this morning, he won't cancel her day's leave. He's got other computer technicians who can stand in for her."

Jordan forced a smile. "It's not exactly proof, is it?"

"Remember when we watched nobody collecting the five million in Kingston Upon Thames? How did Short Circuit know the powers-that-be had coughed up? He – or she – didn't make an appearance in the park." Answering her own question, she continued, "A Unit Red agent would've known what was going on."

"But..."

"What?"

Jordan shook his head. "She can't be getting revenge for Kennington. She didn't know he was in prison – if she told me the truth. But why would anyone go for revenge so long after he's been let out? It's too late."

"Not if sympathy for Eli Kennington isn't the driving force."

Jordan hesitated, thinking. There was another option and its cruelty made him shiver. If Raven really was Short Circuit, she could have taken advantage of Eli Kennington's weakness and innocence. She could have set him up as a stooge. "All right," he said to Kate. "She could've made it look like Kennington by bumping off his enemies. That way, he'd take the blame, not her. But why would she do that?"

Kate let out a long breath and then admitted, "I don't know."

"I suppose it doesn't have to be Raven. Anyone who

knows him could be trying to dump him in it. As long as they're red hot with electronics."

"I guess so."

"Lying here isn't going to sort it out," Jordan said. "I'll get up. It'll take me an age. Do you know how hard it is to get a shirt on with only one hand?"

"Do you want me to...?" She took one look at his frown and grinned. "No, you'd rather take an age than admit you need a woman to dress you." Walking to the door, she said, "I'll leave you to it."

"I'll be down in about eight hours."

Jordan went into the medical room. There, Raven and two technicians were hunched over a single laptop. To the side, Angel and Kate were talking quietly.

"Ah," Angel said, stepping forward. "Sit down. We're ready..."

"As ready as we're ever going to be," Raven said.

"Relax," Angel continued. "They're just going to try turning one system on. Not everything."

"Is that so only one thing cops it, if it goes wrong?"

Angel paused before answering. "I can't lie to you, Jordan. There's a risk. One step at a time is a wise precaution."

"It's a fiendishly tricky program, this," Raven admitted. "But we're going for your sense of smell first."

"Because that's the one I can most easily do without?"

The others looked at each other and then Angel said, "Yes. Let's do it."

Jordan realized that he was holding his breath as one of the technicians typed for a few seconds and then hit the *return* key.

Everyone in the room was gazing at Jordan, waiting.

Nothing clicked in his head or anywhere else. Nothing jolted or went dead. After a few seconds, Jordan smiled, sniffed and said, "Someone stepped in something nasty this morning."

"Wasn't me," Raven replied quickly. "I've been working here all night."

They all checked their shoes. One of the computer specialists said, "It could be me. There's a tiny stain. I can't smell it, but it could be dog mess."

Jordan said, "It got stronger when you lifted your shoe up."

Angel beamed broadly. "The joys of an acute nose."

There were other, nicer smells. Raven hadn't applied her fruity cedar-wood perfume recently, but the characteristic whiff lingered.

"Right," Angel continued. "Visual system. Are you all ready? Jordan?"

"Yes."

His eyesight clarified in an instant. It went from flat grey to full and clear colour, like turning on a TV. But he didn't immediately make sense of the images, as if he'd tuned in to a program showing a bizarre dream sequence. Tints, focus and lustre came and went.

"It might take a while to reboot itself," Angel explained.

The chief was right. After a few seconds, the pictures settled to normal and Jordan sighed with relief.

Angel pointed to the eye-test chart attached to the far wall. "Can you read the bottom line of letters?"

"Easily," Jordan replied. "And underneath, the small print says, 'Made in Loughborough, UK.'"

"Does it?" Angel said, squinting at the testcard. He had to get close to check what Jordan had seen from a distance.

Within another three minutes, all of Jordan's systems were up and running again. Using his false arm and hand, he'd passed Angel's test of picking up a five pence coin from the floor. He turned towards the IT specialists and said, "Thanks, guys."

"You look a lot happier."

"I feel...whole again."

"Right," Angel said emphatically. "Back to work."

"Oh?"

"I got news from the windmill," Angel told Jordan. "There was no sign of a breakout, but Kennington and his car had gone. That means he had a key inside. I guess he just woke up, grabbed it and left."

"I'm surprised he could find it. He had stuff all over the place."

Angel nodded. "The agent's sifting through everything right now. And these technicians are going through his laptop, looking for incriminating evidence."

"No sign of it yet," one of them said.

"But the important point," Angel stressed, "is that Eli Kennington's on the loose again. And we're a day away from Short Circuit's next strike."

Looking up, Raven added, "It could be hours if he strikes just after midnight tonight."

20 GUARDIAN ANGEL

"The trouble with a job like ours," Raven said to Kate, "is that it can become your life, instead of just being part of it." It was lunchtime on Saturday and Raven was about to leave. "I'm on call over the rest of the weekend. Slightest whiff of an emergency and I'll be back in. Let's hope I don't see you till Monday."

"Okay," Kate replied. "Have fun."

As soon as Raven walked out of the room, Kate glanced at her watch. Without telling anyone else what she was going to do, she waited for half an hour and then went to her own car. First, she checked that the transmitter she'd sneaked in to Raven's Volvo was working. Then she eased out of the garage and followed the signal north-east out of London. By tracking Raven, Kate expected to discover once and for all whether her colleague had anything to do with Short Circuit.

Guided by the transmitter, she pulled into a lay-by on a quiet road that cut through Epping Forest. With a puzzled expression, she examined the signal from the transmitter. Raven's Volvo was two hundred metres ahead and it hadn't moved for twenty minutes. Kate looked around. Apart from the narrow road, she was surrounded by dense trees. She would have preferred to have been called to this spot to put out a forest fire. That had its risks, of course, but Unit Red business was more menacing, it seemed to Kate, because its dangers were unseen. Slowly, she opened her car door and emerged into the cool wind. Scanning from side to side, she decided to make her way towards the stationary Volvo on foot.

She walked parallel to the road on a footpath through the forest. There was little noise apart from the occasional passing traffic. After a minute, she saw the distinctive gold colour of Raven's car. Trying to keep to the cover of the trees, she crept nearer and nearer. There was no one in the Volvo. It had been abandoned in the wood. Jumping across a ditch, she came out into the open. Curious, she went up to the car, peered inside and then walked right around it. Stopping by the driver's door, she tried the handle. It wasn't locked and she noticed that the key was in the ignition. She opened the door and glanced about her once more. Still there was no sign of her Unit Red colleague.

Slipping into the driver's seat, she felt underneath the dashboard. The transmitter she'd put there was no longer in place. But it had led her to this quiet spot. Where was it now? Where was Raven and what was she doing?

Kate did not have to wait for answers. She jolted as she realized that Raven was outside, looming over her. Kate opened the window. "Hi. Er... I'm sorry..."

Black hair blowing in the wind and laptop in hand, Raven said, "Thank goodness you're here. Can I borrow your mobile?"

"Er... Yeah. Sure." Kate handed it to her through the window. "What's wrong?"

Raven took it, slipped it into a pocket and replied, "Nothing. At least, nothing's wrong with me. But it'd be a good idea if you stayed right where you are." She pressed a button on the laptop.

"What do you mean?"

"Do you think a computer specialist wouldn't know who's been looking up what at work? Like you checking my holiday dates. And do you think I don't scan my car for bugs? That's very naïve of you. I can tell you're new to this game."

Kate took a deep breath. "I'm new to devious people, for sure."

Raven had the tiny transmitter in her palm. She clenched her hand into a fist and threw the bug into the wood. "No more snooping. Did you tell the others you were after me? I doubt it. You wouldn't admit it in case you looked stupid, sneaky and disloyal."

"I don't think I'm the only one who's sneaky and disloyal."

A silver car zoomed past the lay-by.

"But you're the only one who's been stupid. I knew you'd come to investigate." Raven leaned on the car with her elbow. "We're going to swap cars. I guess yours is just down the lane. And, yes, I came prepared with a key for it. You're driving this one. Go exactly where the SatNav tells you. If you turn it off, stray from the course, push any of its buttons, stop for more than five minutes, or get out the car, the explosives I put in the boot will go up. And you with them."

"What?" The colour drained from Kate's face and her stomach suddenly churned.

"I put a pressure sensor under your seat. It detects the driver's weight so it knows you're sitting there. I've connected it to the bomb in the boot. Quite close to the fuel tank. If you take your weight off the seat...boom."

"But..."

"You look petrified," Raven said with a smile.

"Why are you doing this?"

"Unit Red wasn't the only secret organization that recruited me." It wasn't really an answer to the question, but Raven gave no further explanation. She looked down at her watch. "Did I tell you the clock started ticking down one-and-a-half minutes ago? I wouldn't hang around if I were you. Five minutes without moving and then you've had it."

Kate tried to come to terms with her terrifying situation. "What if I get in a hold-up?"

"You won't. It's a high-class SatNav. It's online, scanning for jams. If it detects any, it'll route you round them."

"What happens when I get where I'm going – wherever that is?"

"The SatNav signal will override the pressure sensor. You get out and open the boot. If anyone tries to get into the boot before that, the car goes skywards. You'll see a hand-held computer on standby next to the detonator. Hit the *return* key twice. That disables the bomb and let's you get away safely."

Kate hesitated, certain that she hadn't heard the whole story. "That can't be all. The computer button does something else as well, doesn't it?"

Raven tapped the face of her watch. "Coming up for two-and-a-half minutes. If you don't want to die right here, you'd better get cracking."

Kate held out her hand.

"What?" Raven asked.

"My mobile."

Raven laughed. "No chance. You're on your own. That's why I took it off you."

"Jordan was right," Kate muttered. "You *are* Short Circuit."

Denied any real choice, Kate drove away in the car that would kill her if she deviated, stopped for more than five minutes, or got out.

At once, the male voice from the SatNav directed her on to the A414 towards Chelmsford. The voice was deceptively soothing. It packed a powerful punch if Kate dared to disobey. At least, that's what Raven had told her and there was no safe way to find out if it was true.

Kate could do nothing but follow instructions.

Coming up to the traffic island in Ongar, she braked. On her left, a group of young people were hanging out in front of a garage forecourt. And that gave her an idea.

She pulled over to the side of the road, opened the passenger's electric window and leaned towards it while keeping all her weight on her own seat. "Hey!" she shouted out of the window. "Who's got a crap mobile?"

The kids looked at each other and then one boy stepped forward. "What do you mean?"

"I need one in a hurry," she replied. Fiddling in her purse, she said, "I can give you sixty quid. That's all I've got."

A girl came up to the window and waved a cheap pink phone at her. "Sixty for that?"

Kate nodded. "Sure. I'd pay double if I had it."

The girl could hardly believe her luck. She glanced at the others and then said, "Okay. It's yours. Give me a second to delete some things."

Kate counted the banknotes again and held them out. "I don't have long," she said, "and I don't care about your stuff. I won't even look. Leave it switched on. I just need to make an important call."

"Sixty quid," the boy said. "That's a steep call."

"Yeah, I know," Kate agreed. "But..."

The girl leaned through the open window, took the money and handed over her mobile. With a wide grin on her face, she said, "Good deal."

Kate nodded. "For both of us. Thanks."

She accelerated away into the stream of traffic. Keeping an eye on the road, she dialled the Unit Red crisis number. Hoping there were no traffic cops in the area, she put the phone to her ear with one hand and steered with the other.

Jordan and Angel were listening to Kate's call on a loudspeaker in the bunker. "Hang on, hang on," Angel interrupted with a look of horror and surprise on his face. "Are you saying Raven...?"

"Yes, she's Short Circuit. Ask Jordan. He knows all about it. But, right now, I'm driving a bomb somewhere. Somewhere I don't know. I think I'm going to wreck something or someone when I get there – or on the way. I should've refused to drive," Kate said miserably. "That way, the car would've blown up and I would've taken her with me."

"I would've got going as well," Jordan told her.

Angel put aside the shock that swept over him so he

could deal with the situation. "No one here doubts your bravery, Kate," he said. "You don't sacrifice yourself when there's a chance..."

"What am I going to do, though?"

"Keep driving. We'll lock on to your mobile and track your position. Before we make any decisions, let's see where you're going."

Jordan said, "You can use the SatNav to find out where it's taking you."

"No, I can't," she replied. "The bomb goes up if I touch it."

Angel paused for a moment, thinking. "All right. Drive slowly, Kate. I'm going to put Jordan in a helicopter. I can have him airborne in twenty minutes. He'll be above you, ready to help."

"I don't want to kill anyone else," said Kate, her voice wavering.

"I'm used to explosions," Jordan replied. "They've never finished me off yet. I'm on my way."

The motorcycle rider wove expertly round the Saturday afternoon traffic, on the way to London Heliport. Clinging on tightly behind him, Jordan wondered why he hadn't been trained to ride a bike himself. The journey to

Battersea would have taken him four times longer by car, bus or Underground.

A woman in a high-visibility jacket met him in the car park and ran with him to the helipad perched on the southern edge of the Thames. As soon as he was strapped in to the waiting chopper and given a headset, the pilot left the ground. Almost at once, the helicopter rose above the height of the tallest buildings – all curves and glass – and soon left them far below. The office blocks became stiff fingers, pointing up at Jordan. Battersea Park was a splodge of green among the bricks and concrete. At its far side was the unmistakable Battersea Power Station. Wasting no time, the motorized bubble lurched north-east. Next to Jordan, the pilot soon had the chopper on full throttle, speeding towards Essex.

"Going round Chelmsford," Kate's voice said hesitantly. "Turning onto the A12 towards Colchester, Ipswich and Felixstowe."

Inside Jordan's helmet, speakers fed sound to his ears. He could hear every conversation involving Angel, Kate or the pilot. The tiny microphone that bent round in front of his mouth allowed him to speak to them all.

"Yes," Angel replied. "We're still locked on."

"Copy," the pilot said. "We'll be joining you as soon as possible."

"Is the phone battery okay?" Angel asked Kate. "It's not going to die a death soon, is it?"

There was a delay of a few seconds. "Two bars of power left," she replied. "I guess that'll do for a few hours."

The helicopter followed the Thames for a few minutes and then flew over the brand new Olympic Park. Jordan's whole body felt the vibrations from the rotors and, despite the muffling effect of the headset, there was a constant loud drone in his hearing system. "Can't we go any faster?" he asked the pilot.

"No. Our forward speed is just over two hundred kilometres an hour. That's tops for this model."

"How long before we catch her up?"

"She's leaving Chelmsford so we're about sixty kilometres behind. If she's taking it easy on sixty or seventy kilometres an hour, we'll be above her in...er... half an hour."

"Let's hope it's soon enough."

Sensing Jordan's anxiety, the pilot kept pointing out features on the ground to stress how quickly they were leaving London behind. "Romford," he said, jabbing his finger downwards. Later, he said, "The M25. Brentwood ahead. We're in Essex. That ribbon's the A12."

The county looked even flatter than it really was. Toy

towns and villages broke up the regular patchwork of fields. The next landmark was Chelmsford. The pilot kept to the southern edge, following the bypass.

"Everything okay, Kate?" Angel asked.

A long way ahead of the helicopter, she answered, "No change. Still on the same road." Her voice sounded strained.

"You're doing great," Angel said. "Try to hold your nerve and stay calm."

"If you don't turn off, we'll join you at Colchester," the pilot informed her.

"That's good," she replied. "I could use the company, even if you're way over my head." She hesitated before adding, "I could use a guardian angel."

"Never been called that before," Jordan said with a grin. His smile soon faded. Even if the pilot landed close to Kate, Jordan didn't know what he could do. He'd joked about surviving explosions but really he dreaded another. He'd already lost his family to one massive blast. He couldn't stand the thought of losing anyone else that way. He also feared further pain and injuries.

For another ten minutes, the ground slid underneath Jordan. The pilot pointed ahead and said into his microphone, "Approaching Colchester now. Update your position, please, Kate."

"Just going past a golf course on my right, still on the A12."

"We're close behind you."

"What sort of car is it?" Jordan asked. "I never knew what Raven drove."

"It's a Volvo S60."

"What colour?"

"Gold."

The pilot came in on the exchange. "I'm going to come in low – as low as I'm allowed. If you hear a helicopter or see us, wave something out of the window. It'll help us pinpoint you."

"Okay."

The chopper swooped and Jordan felt his stomach lurch as if he were on a fairground ride. He ignored the unsettling feeling as the ground seemed to rush up at him. Gazing forwards and down, he soon began to make out individual vehicles on the dual carriageway as it bypassed the centre of Colchester. He picked out huge rumbling lorries first. He couldn't distinguish one make of car from another, but he could tell small from large. Sunshine glinting on the cars made it difficult to distinguish one colour from another, but he could tell light from dark.

"I'm going over a road but there isn't a junction onto

it," said Kate. "Just a second." After a few moments, she added, "The SatNav says I'm coming up to a junction in two kilometres. I'm going to bear right to stay on the A12. Have you seen me yet, Jordan?"

"No, but we must be close." He could see a swirl of roads ahead. It had to be the junction.

"A big green lorry's going past me right now."

Frantically, Jordan scanned his field of view on maximum strength. "Yes," he cried. "I think..."

"I'll wave out of the widow."

"Yes," Jordan confirmed. "Got you."

The pilot glanced across at him, perhaps surprised by the power of his sight. "Keep your eye on her."

Guessing that the pilot didn't know he had enhanced vision, Jordan pointed towards the gold S60.

"Going in closer," the pilot announced.

"Okay," Angel's voice said. "Everything's in place. All we need is a destination and a plan."

21 SKY HIGH

Jordan didn't really need Kate to tell him where she was, but she kept up a running commentary anyway. "Going round Ipswich ring road... Coming up to the Felixstowe turning... I wonder... Wait. No... I'm back on the A12, heading for Woodbridge."

"All these places are familiar to Short Circuit," said Angel.

"Everyone prefers to play at home," Kate replied. She drove faster now, perhaps eager to end the whole experience.

There wasn't much to say for the next twenty-seven kilometres, but then Kate broke radio silence. "The SatNav's just told me to take the next right. It's a minor road. The B1121 for Saxmundham and Leiston."

Angel's voice was suddenly urgent. "Right. I know where you're going and it's bad news. It's not going to be Saxmundham or Leiston. Sizewell's just beyond them."

The pilot said, "The nuclear power station?"

"Bound to be," Angel replied. "So we've got to intervene. She'll turn right onto the B1119 any second now. Fly on ahead and find somewhere to land near the road. I need Jordan on the ground. Make sure it's well short of Sizewell. Kate: we can't let you near a nuclear facility with a bomb. The threat's too great."

"I know," Kate replied quietly.

"For the good of everyone," Angel continued, "we can't have a nuclear incident. It'd be a disaster. If necessary, Kate..."

"Yes," she said, interrupting. "I may have to veer off course."

Jordan shuddered as he heard her acceptance of Angel's chilling verdict. The acceptance of her own death. She was prepared to sacrifice herself to save thousands.

"Not yet," Angel said. "Drive slowly. Let's see what Jordan can come up with. And I'll send in a bomb-disposal team as soon as I can get one. Now, give me a moment to talk to the people who run the power station. I've got to alert them. Just in case."

The nuclear complex loomed large ahead of Jordan, on the boundary between land and sea. The site contained several uninspiring rectangular buildings and one huge white dome that looked like a giant golf ball.

Below them was a village. On a square field next to a school was the largest bouncy castle that Jordan had ever seen. Kids were swarming over it. To the side, some fairground rides were lined up on the recreation ground. None of the people there realized that they were in great danger. They were busy enjoying themselves.

The pilot said, "There's a construction site by the road on the outskirts. No one'll be working on a Saturday. I can put her down on the foundations of whatever they're building. A short run will take you to the road to Sizewell."

"What's the village?"

"Leiston."

Jordan nodded. "Kate. Look out for a building site when you leave Leiston. I'll be waiting."

"What are you going to do?" she asked.

"I don't know."

She paused for a second and then replied, "Just when

I need some reassurance... Honesty's not always the best policy."

"Stop on the road," he told her. "Don't take a turn."

"We'll have five minutes before the car goes up."

"Five minutes to get you out, run to the chopper and take off."

"No luck with a bomb squad," Angel reported. "You're on your own. Sizewell's still operational but it's gone into lockdown. No one in or out."

That would stop a bomb, Jordan thought, but locking doors and gates wouldn't stop an electrical signal triggering a hardware Trojan or a cyber attack. It wouldn't stop an electronic meltdown.

Kate must have been thinking the same thing because she said, "I'm worried about what's in the boot. A bomb and a computer, if we believe Raven. She might've primed the computer. It might send a signal to the power station that shuts it down or makes it go wrong. That'd be typical for Short Circuit."

Doing his best to sound confident, Jordan replied, "Maybe. But I'm going to get you out and let the bomb blow up anything else in the boot."

As soon as the landing skids touched the concrete base, Jordan pulled off his headset and safety strap. He jumped down and made for the lane out of the village.

It was the road that connected Leiston to the nuclear site at Sizewell.

He didn't have to wait for long. The gold Volvo cruised up to him and came to a stop.

On the phone, Kate had given the impression of being calm and in control, but she looked haggard. "There's a pressure sensor in the seat. If I get up..."

"Yeah, you told us." Unsure, Jordan looked around.

"Don't do anything with the boot. But Raven didn't say anything about the other doors."

Luckily, the road was quiet on a Saturday. There was no other traffic.

Jordan dashed round to the passenger's side and opened the door. Making up his mind, he said, "Right. I'm going to fetch some bricks and stuff. Anything heavy. I'll dump it on your seat so you can edge out slowly while this stuff makes up the weight."

First, he grabbed a stack of bricks. He used the strength of his right arm to haul them back to the car and his left arm to steady the pile.

"Okay," he said to his partner. "Budge up a bit. Give me enough room to load these onto your seat."

Kate was sweating. She realized that one wrong move could kill both of them. She leaned slightly to the right while Jordan put the first three bricks on the seat, against her thigh. "How much weight will fool the sensor?"

Jordan looked at her blankly. "There's only one honest answer."

"You don't know."

"Right," he said, loading more bricks on top of the others.

Kate glanced at her watch. "I didn't check the time when I got here. How long have we got?"

"I'm online, monitoring the time. A minute-and-a-half. We're all right for now, but..."

"But?"

"I think I need something heavier." He looked around again. "Like that." He ran across the road to a heap of big bags filled with cement. Each one was twenty five kilograms. Steeling himself, he picked up the top one and lugged it back to the car. Bending over, he lifted the heavy yet floppy bag awkwardly over the passenger seat and handbrake. He almost threw it against Kate's side.

She didn't grumble. She shuffled further to the right to make room for the sack.

"One more to make sure," he said breathlessly. "That'll be up to your weight."

Kate smiled through her anxiety, attempting to stay cool. "Very flattering."

Jordan tried not to think about what would happen if he got this wrong. Taking a deep breath, he hoisted another sack of cement onto his artificial arm. As quickly as he could, he staggered back to the Volvo.

Three minutes and fifteen seconds had passed since Kate had stopped the car.

"Right," he said to her. "When I slap this one down, you jump out. Okay?"

"What if it doesn't work?"

He smiled at her. "It will. Don't worry."

"Honest?"

"No problem." But he felt the sweat rolling down his own face now.

"Okay."

In the background, the helicopter's engine revved.

"When you jump out, don't stop. Run. We've got a minute and a bit to get away." He looked into her face and asked, "Ready?"

She took a breath. "Ready."

"Go!" Jordan shouted.

As Kate eased out, he thrust the second sack of cement onto the seat.

And nothing happened. There was no explosion.

Jordan didn't stop to celebrate. He scrambled out and began to follow Kate towards the helicopter. The bomb in the boot was due to detonate in just over a minute.

But movement in the lane distracted him. Three boys – much younger than Jordan – were cycling down the lane towards the car. Perhaps they'd seen or heard the chopper and had come to investigate.

As Kate swung herself up into the chopper, Jordan stopped, changed course and raced towards the boys. Waving his arms, he yelled, "Get away from here!"

"Why?"

"This is our road," the second one said.

"Who are you to tell us what to do?"

Jordan didn't have time to explain or argue. He slid to a halt by a speed limit sign. It was there to slow vehicles entering the village. He swung his right arm at the pole and it buckled at once. The road sign bowed its head in submission. "Turn round and go back or I'll rip your heads off."

The boys stared at the damage he'd done to the metal post, and then at Jordan. A split second later, they turned and pedalled away as quickly as they could.

Jordan sprinted towards the chopper. Its engine was roaring, overloading his hearing system. Its rotor blades were at full power, kicking up sand and cement. Jordan fought his way through the dust storm. Seeing that the helicopter was already hovering off the ground, he put on a final burst of speed and launched himself at the open door.

His left ankle hit the landing skid, his knee caught the muffler and he didn't quite make it. As the chopper rose steeply, Kate reached out to grab him, but she wasn't quick enough and she couldn't get a grip. He fell.

22 EXTREME VIOLENCE

He didn't fall far. Jordan's mechanical fingers clamped round the landing skid. The weight of his body jolted the bolt attached to the bones of his shoulder, but he clung on tightly. He dangled in mid-air as the pilot continued to surge upwards and away. Jordan knew the helicopter wouldn't descend even though he was in great danger. If the pilot swooped down when the bomb activated, it would be much worse for Jordan. He had to hold on.

But Jordan's online brain told him it was now six minutes since Kate had parked the car in the lane that led to Sizewell B nuclear power station. He didn't dare to look down, but he knew that the Volvo was still in one piece. He hadn't heard an explosion or felt the shock wave.

The helicopter was circling over the village of Leiston, but keeping clear of the building site. The pilot was probably deciding what to do, consulting with Angel perhaps.

Jordan didn't need to be told the decision. The chopper flew lower and lower, heading for the centre of Leiston. The children playing on the bouncy castle scattered as the helicopter descended and hovered above it. Jordan looked down. About fifteen metres below him, the bouncy surface was now deserted but it seemed a long way down. Taking a deep breath, he let go of the skid and plummeted through the air. When he thudded into the cushioned castle, the wobbly walls folded in momentarily and belched loudly, like an old man. Then the whole structure let out a long wheezing sigh. The force of Jordan's landing had punctured it.

At once, the helicopter moved away. Unhurt, Jordan scrambled off the castle as it slowly sagged. He looked around the startled faces of the children and their parents and said, "Sorry about that." He wasn't sure of his next move, but he knew he should get away. Once the villagers recovered from the shock of his sudden gate-crashing of their fair, they could turn ugly.

His mobile rang. It was Angel. "The pilot's going to bring the chopper down at Leiston Abbey. He says he's done it before. It's just to the north. Two kilometres at most. Up Abbey Road, appropriately enough."

"What about Raven's car?"

"Leave it. The local police are nearly there and a Sizewell team's about to take a look. It'll probably be a controlled explosion. We're not taking any chances."

Jordan's inertial navigation system told him which way was north. He jogged from the recreation ground and went to the left. "Is Sizewell okay?"

"Yes," Angel said. "No electrical interference. I've got you on my monitor, by the way. You're moving in the right direction."

"I can hear the helicopter," Jordan replied. He didn't need to be guided. He simply homed in on the sound of the rotor blades.

When he reached the chopper, Kate offered him her hand and yanked him up into the remaining seat.

While Jordan fastened his safety belt and put on a helmet, the helicopter rose, turned and headed south-west. Leiston and Sizewell disappeared below and behind them.

As soon as he'd settled, Jordan heard Kate's voice in his earpiece. "That makes us quits."

"How come?" he replied.

"I saved you. Now you've saved me."

Jordan twisted towards her. "But I didn't. The bomb didn't go off."

"You didn't know it wouldn't."

"Still not sure it counts," Jordan said.

By the time Jordan and Kate got back to Highgate, an expert had dealt with Raven's abandoned Volvo. "There weren't any explosives," Angel told them in the bunker. "It was all a great big hoax."

Kate sighed and shook her head. "She sent me on a wild goose chase."

"It wasn't your fault," Angel said to her. "You couldn't have known. Assuming the worst was the only thing you could do and, anyway, no one got hurt."

"She must have distracted us for a reason," Kate muttered.

"I hate to say it, but maybe she's trying to prove she can run rings around us. Or perhaps she's having a laugh at our expense. Like she did with the money in Kingston."

"I bet she won't be kidding next time she goes into action," said Jordan.

Angel nodded. "I agree. It'll be for real tomorrow."

"But where? And what?"

"Well," Kate said, "we know it won't be Sizewell."

"I need to understand what's driving her." Angel sounded frustrated. "Any ideas?"

"I thought she was getting back at everyone involved in Eli Kennington's trial," Jordan replied. "She said she didn't know he'd been in prison, but she must have been lying."

Angel frowned. "Lying's the least of her crimes."

"I don't think it's right anyway," Jordan said. "More likely, she set him up to take the blame."

Recalling the conversation in Epping Forest, Kate told them, "She said something about being in a secret organization."

Angel gazed at her. "What sort of organization? Did she say?"

Kate shook her head. "Afraid not."

"How did she join Unit Red?" Jordan asked.

"I keep my eye on universities for any bright kids coming through the system. That's how I spotted her. If all goes well, there's a right time to welcome someone special like Raven into Unit Red. You know this," he said, looking at Jordan. "You weren't on my radar until the Thames Estuary explosion, but I swooped afterwards – when the time was right. Raven got a job at HiSpec, got booted out – unfairly – and, at her lowest ebb, I turned up next to her in the pub."

"You knew she'd worked at HiSpec?"

"Yes. I also knew why she tried to hide it and I let her think she'd been successful. Maybe..." Angel stopped. He wasn't going to admit he'd misjudged the situation. Instead, he told them, "She had a troubled childhood. When she was young, she had no time for anything but computer games. Her schooling suffered. Her mum and dad always compared her unfavourably with her brother – a high-flier at school. Apparently, they used to tell her she was worthless and lazy. They said she'd never get a job and earn money. You can imagine the resentment. And the anger. One day, she snapped and burned her house down, but she didn't realize her big brother was inside. Her parents went in to rescue him. None of them came out alive."

"Not a deliberate killing, then?" said Kate.

"Unlikely. But you can probably imagine the headlines as well. 'Little Monster Murders Family' and so on. She was way below the age of criminal responsibility. For her own protection, she was given a new identity – Madison Flint – and adopted."

"So even that isn't her real name," Jordan said.

"No," Angel replied. "But her new parents recognized her genius and she came on in leaps and bounds. She was a lot happier, so it's possible the young Madison Flint learned that extreme violence pays off. It destroyed a bad family and gave her a much more understanding one."

Kate asked, "What are her latest bouts of extreme violence supposed to achieve?"

Neither Jordan nor Angel had an answer.

On cue, Angel's computer chirped to announce the arrival of another audio file. This time, Short Circuit hadn't doctored the sound. There was no point. Jordan, Kate and Angel recognized Raven's voice straight away.

I know how it works. I bet you're having a meeting – probably in the bunker. Trying to figure me out.

I don't know the first thing about explosives. I'd probably blow myself up if I tried to do anything with them. No. Working with electronics isn't as showy, but it's far easier and much more deadly.

As you've found out, I was joking about the bomb in the boot.

Jordan's sound system picked out background noises. He heard the Lemon Jelly song playing very quietly. There was also the roar of an aeroplane's jet engine. Short Circuit was clearly toying with them. Again.

When Stryker took the case on, he asked me to find out if Short Circuit had had a practice run before bringing the planes down. Barking up the wrong tree. It's all been a practice run for what I've got in mind. And it's nothing to do with Eli Kennington and his trial.

I knew Kennington had been behind bars. I also found out he put hardware Trojans in HiSpec's chips – for fun and challenge, I suppose. He's pathetic. No malicious intent at all. He wouldn't do anything to get his own back. What a waste of technology. So I hijacked his Trojans for my own ends. But it took me a while to figure out how to use them.

To be honest, trying to control Paige Ottaway's robotic laser was a complete flop. It all went horribly wrong. The Trojans I activated went into overdrive and killed her. I had no control at all, so I went back to basics. I hit a couple of planes. Big targets, easy jobs. Just had to stop some circuits in the flight systems and down they came.

But I'm ambitious. I still needed to step up a gear. I had to work out how to make circuit boards do what I wanted. Once I'd cracked it, I fine-tuned my methods on the people who'd put Kennington away so he'd take the rap if anything went wrong. I even tried to mimic his weird way of talking on the sound clips.

I got control for the first time when I persuaded a Trojan in Victoria Truman's automated system to turn her gas on and another in Edward Jackson's pacemaker to shock his heart. But I wanted to test myself with another form of transport. Stryker's Jag came to mind, but I didn't want to do it under your nose, so I went to Ipswich. I wasn't really trying to get Lazenby but – I could hardly believe my luck – Stryker put him in the Jag.

I was going to carry on with everyone who'd played a part in getting Kennington jailed, but you got too close, especially when you locked him up in his holiday cottage and sent someone over to talk to him. That would have been...awkward.

Made me pleased I'd brought my plans forward.
I'm ready.

There was a gap of a few seconds. Angel didn't turn the audio file off, though, because he could see that it had not finished.

You think you know everything about your agents, Angel. You think you know everything about me. But you don't. I got introduced to a mixed bag of people who believe society in this country needs overturning. They think we should step back from the relentless pursuit of money and goods. Life shouldn't be about owning the next gadget.

Strange thing for a computer geek to say? I love computers because they're under our control. They help us do things. But what's the next generation of gadgets? It's all about cybernetics, artificial intelligence, robotic soldiers. They'll get out of our control. That sort of technology is a step too far. It's a danger to all our futures.

In a way, I'm the opposite of Eli Kennington. He can't wait for the singularity. I dread it so much I'm going to do everyone a favour and stop it happening. Now you know why I never liked Stryker. It isn't anything to do with terahertz technology. It's about what he is.

"She's been brainwashed," Angel muttered.

Actually, bringing a plane down on the Houses of Parliament was another one of our attempts to destabilize the country. Pity Stryker got in the way. Anyway, you wouldn't believe how pleased the group is to have me. An agent with the computer skills to force a change of direction. You also won't believe what's coming next.

The clip ended and Angel let out a snort. "I need to listen to that again, but we're no closer to what she's doing."

"Or where she is," Jordan added.

Brightening up, Kate said, "Don't forget she's in my car. If we can find it..."

"Already done," Angel replied. "It was abandoned in central London. I'm having it towed back. Interestingly, three cars were stolen within five kilometres of it. Maybe Raven nicked one of them. It doesn't tell us where she is now, but I've got someone tracing all three."

Unsure whether he was about to make a fool of himself, Jordan said, "I can't help thinking about something Amy Goss once told me." For Kate's benefit, he explained, "She was my best friend at school and her dad was big in crime. He got away with a robbery years ago. His men broke into a bank vault and stole a lot of money. The police never found it. They put it somewhere really clever and used it bit by bit."

"Where?" Angel asked, intrigued by Jordan's story.

"In the bank they nicked it from. Is it called a safe deposit box or something?"

"Yes."

"That's where they put it. In Mr. Goss's safe deposit box in the vault they'd just smashed their way into."

Angel gazed at him. "And your point is?"

"It was a sort of double bluff – and it worked."

"What are you saying?" Kate asked.

"Maybe Raven *is* targeting the nuclear power station at Sizewell. Because she's already pretended to have a go at it, it's the one place we wouldn't expect her to choose."

"I can't base my tactics on a hunch like that," Angel said.

The secure phone rang and Angel answered it immediately. At first he simply listened, his face fixed with concentration. Then he responded, "Follow up the burned-out one." Putting the phone down and looking at Kate, he said, "Those stolen cars. One's been found burned out, another's not been traced and one's in police hands after a high-speed chase with a joyrider. Raven would be careful to destroy evidence so, if she did take one of them, she might well have torched it once she'd finished with it."

"Where did they find it?"

"Still in London. South of the river. Not near any obvious target." He glanced at the clock. "Besides, it's too early. She's going to strike sometime after midnight. Sunday 27th May is what she said." He shook his head. "Do you know what I think we're going to need?"

Jordan reckoned he was on Angel's wavelength. "Help with computing?"

"Exactly. We need the best."

Jordan nodded. "Someone like Eli Kennington."

Angel smiled. "Not someone like him. We need the real thing. Go and find him, Kate, and then reel him in. Don't tell him who we are, but promise him anything you like. Just get him."

23 TOO LATE

The sun sank behind Highgate Cemetery and nocturnal animals took over from tourists, prowling between the old gravestones. Above them, bats circled around the open space, picking off insects. Saturday night seemed to be lasting for ever, like history lessons when Jordan was the schoolboy Ben Smith. Now, it was tension rather than boredom that made time expand. Without knowing what Raven was doing and where she was, there was nothing that he could do. Apart from wait. He was waiting for the end of civilization – or whatever she was planning – instead of preventing it. And that frustrated him.

Jordan Stryker had been built for threats like this – built for action – and he was lounging around, watching the figures on the digital clock transform every second.

Saturday became Sunday and there was still no news, no sightings of Raven, no action. It crossed Jordan's mind that, in telling them she was planning chaos some time today, Raven could be bluffing once more. But Jordan had a feeling that this time she wasn't. She'd perfected her attacks. She was all set.

It was well after dawn when Angel took the call from one of his agents. Immediately, he turned to Jordan. "Right. This is the best we've got. Another car went missing a few kilometres away from that burned-out wreck and it's just been picked up on the CCTV of an engineering company next to Gatwick Airport. It smells like Raven to me, covering her tracks by switching cars on her way to a target. Remember she said she wanted to practise on forms of transport – like your car? Maybe it's a Gatwick plane next. Get on the road, Jordan. I'll send the postcode to your inertial navigation system."

Jordan nodded and made for the door.

"Take care," Angel said. "Raven is devious and determined."

* * *

The plain flat-roofed building belonged to an engineering company. It stood at the end of a private lane, positioned on the perimeter of Gatwick Airport. From the top of its two storeys flew a large Union flag. The upper level appeared to consist of offices. The ground floor of the building was tall and cluttered with machinery. On a Sunday, it was devoid of workers, but outside a solitary car stood in the large parking area. It looked out of place.

"Yes," Jordan whispered into his phone. "The car's here. No sign of anyone, though."

The voice in his ear replied, "Proceed with caution."

Somewhere behind the factory, an aeroplane's engines roared. By the time Jordan saw the plane, it was climbing into the sky on its way to some distant destination. He thought of Ecuador and Edinburgh.

Walking up to the factory's main entrance, he looked through a window. He could make out nothing but earth-moving equipment, scaffolding components, concrete mixers and a lot of other heavy machinery. There was no movement. He couldn't see into the upper storey.

The entrance did not appear to have been forced open. It was firmly locked. The huge sliding door – used to get the bulky items in and out – was also intact and secure. Jordan went to the right and began to walk round the brick-built factory. Turning the corner, he saw a large field beyond the sturdy wire fence. It belonged to the airport. Another plane was now hurtling along the runway, not yet off the ground. The tall fence was topped with vicious razor wire.

The side door bore a large sign. *Staff Only*. Like the entry at the front, it was intact and did not respond to Jordan's pushing and pulling. If Raven was inside the works, maybe she'd got hold of a key.

To Jordan's enhanced power of smell, the whole area reeked of fumes from aviation fuel. Against a background of aircraft coming and going at regular intervals, he continued his examination of the factory. The back of the building – the wall nearest to the airport enclosure – was almost entirely brickwork. It was decorated only by graffiti and a narrow door. But this one had been levered open. The wooden frame bore the marks of a crowbar and the door itself was dented around the lock.

"Someone's forced their way in," Jordan reported quietly. "I'm checking it out."

The ground floor was oddly still and sinister, filled with strange giant shapes. Girders and cranes reached up and out like huge framework arms, metallic and rigid.

Jordan's footfalls echoed around the vast space. Even with his hearing on maximum, the drone of aircraft and his own footsteps were the only sounds that he could detect.

He made for the aluminium steps up to the offices. Perhaps, if Raven was somewhere among the machinery on the ground floor, he'd spot her from high up on the stairs.

He placed his foot silently on the metallic grid that formed the first step and eased himself up quietly. He didn't place his right hand on the aluminium banister in case it made a clunking sound. He continued up the stairs slowly and noiselessly.

From halfway up, he hung over the rail and surveyed the works below. Using visible and infrared wavelengths, he saw no evidence of anyone else. Everything was colder than a human being so his night vision detected only dull blues and greys. There was no telltale glow from a warm body.

Taking a deep breath, he carried on cautiously to the top of the framework steps.

The upper storey wasn't divided into small rooms. There was a corridor leading to two massive open-plan offices. At a glance, both were empty of people. If Raven was in the building, she could have concealed herself behind a photocopier, desk or partition. She could even be hiding in a cupboard. Jordan's terahertz vision didn't reveal anything and he couldn't hear the distinctive sound of breathing.

At the end of the corridor, there was a ladder leading up to a hatch in the ceiling. Before he searched the offices more carefully, he decided to poke his head out, just in case Raven had gone out onto the roof.

He grasped the rails and climbed the rungs. Noting that the bolts were undone, he pushed open the hatch. The flat roof had a thick plastic waterproof coating. At the end of a long pole in the centre of the structure, the flag flapped noisily in the wind. Beyond was a clear view of the whole airport. An Airbus lifted off the ground and rose steeply into the blue sky and scattered cloud. With her back to Jordan, Raven watched it go. Just like the flag, her long black hair streamed out behind her.

It was windy, but not windy enough to make the roof scary and dangerous. His heart racing, Jordan clambered quietly onto the flat surface and tiptoed towards her. He hoped the scream of the receding jet would cover the sound of his footsteps as he prepared for the final confrontation, as he prepared to grab Short Circuit.

He'd taken only four steps when she called out, "Ah. My cyber workmate. I wondered when you'd find me.

Too late, as far as you're concerned." Without turning, she pointed downwards. "The Jag's a bit of a giveaway."

There were only two cars in the parking area. The morning sunlight glinted on the black metallic surface of his XJ Sentinel.

Jordan froze and muttered under his breath. She'd known he was there all along. Even so, he sensed the end of his mission. Physically, she was no match for an enhanced agent. For the first time, he stripped away her clothing with his terahertz vision. She wasn't even carrying a hidden weapon.

Before he could take another step, though, he felt as if a light had gone out in his head. He blinked and gulped. He was no longer online. He was isolated and light-headed. And he no longer picked up the smell of aviation fuel.

Raven turned to face him. She had a small computer in her left hand and she was typing with her right. One by one, she was disabling his enhancements, just like Eli Kennington had done in Cambridge.

Next, his robotic arm slammed against his side. No longer a limb, it was a lifeless piece of metal.

Raven had no need of a gun or a knife. In her hands, a computer was a very effective weapon. She was about to click another button, but she stopped herself. "You can keep your hearing and vision. They're no threat to me. That way, you can see and hear the planes coming in and taking off. They're a miracle of modern engineering, aren't they? They're so big, it's amazing they ever get off the ground. From up here," she said, "you get a direct line-of-sight view of the whole airport."

"You're using Eli's hardware Trojans again, aren't you? That's why you need to be near the runway. To activate them with a radio signal."

"You don't have to be a genius to work that out."

"What are you going to do?" he asked.

She closed the lid of her laptop. "Wrong question. It's already done."

"What is?"

"I learned a lot by crashing those first two planes and even more when I took over control systems. Two different skills. Now I'm combining them. Out there," she said, nodding towards Gatwick, "two of the planes that are about to take off will switch to autopilot once they're away from the airport. That's what I've just programmed them to do and the pilots won't be able to get control back. They'll divert to the destination I've locked into their flight and control systems. Both will arrive at the same time. Actually, one would do the job, but it's good to have backup, isn't it? Just in case."

"Where?"

"Wait and find out. Or work it out for yourself. But they'll wish they'd never got off the ground." She walked towards the hatch and said, "You're useless without your enhancements, aren't you?"

Jordan's GPS probably wasn't working any more, but Angel knew exactly where he was. He hoped that Kate was on her way, so Jordan needed to keep Raven talking for as long as possible. "You started out on Paige Ottaway's medical robot."

"Yes?"

"But it was you who first told me about Paige Ottaway. You must have been confident that I wouldn't nail you or you'd have kept quiet. Maybe you thought you'd look guilty if I found out about her later and you hadn't told me."

She shrugged. "I didn't care much. I set Kennington up. If you got close to cracking the case, I knew you'd go after him, not me. I told you: it's good to have a safety net."

He said, "But you deleted all the details of his trial – like the jury list."

"Think about it," Raven replied. "I didn't want to make it too easy. If Kennington had been behind everything, he would've wiped the trial details, so I did as well."

"You've been twisting and turning all along, haven't you?"

She smiled sweetly. "I've thrown a few distractions into the ring."

"You've been brainwashed into it by terrorists."

"I've had a rubbish life. A rubbish family for sure. I had a job then lost it. I had a boyfriend and then lost him. After I joined Unit Red, there wasn't any time for him, so he walked away. Too many sacrifices."

For an instant, Jordan thought about his own sacrifices. He'd lost his family, his place at normal school and, after his first mission, his best friend.

"I suppose I'm showing my contempt for community – and the way it's going," she said. "Those terrorists – as you called them – welcomed me with open arms. We don't see eye-to-eye on everything, it's true, but one message is loud and clear. It's about the type of society we want. We've become dehumanized. Look at you. Part human, part robot. It's going too far. It's about tearing down what we've got and building something better."

"But..."

"No more. Your GPS will have told the others where you are. I'm not hanging around to take on the lot of you. I've got a busy day. Don't think the planes are the only thing I'm doing today. They're just the starting pistol."

"What?"

"There's a cybernetics factory. Maybe even HiSpec," she said, plainly teasing him. "After all, they're supplying the microchips."

Desperate to detain her, he said, "Why don't you kill me?"

She smiled. "I want the powers-that-be to see you fail. I want them – and you – to see robotics isn't the answer."

"If you can beat me with hardware Trojans, you'll always be able to stop machines taking over, won't you?"

She shook her head. "If only. The old spiked chips will be replaced. Design will be tightened up. No more Trojans." Tapping her watch, she took some more steps towards the opening that led down to the offices. "You're trying to delay me, hoping the cavalry will arrive. It won't work. And, yes, both planes will have taken off by now." She disappeared into the hole and, before Jordan could reach it, she slammed down the hatch and bolted it from inside.

To Jordan, it felt as if she'd retreated to the safety of a submarine and locked him outside to face the cruel waves without a means of escape.

He assumed she'd make her getaway in the stolen car. He had to find a way to follow her, but he was hampered by an uncooperative body. He went right to the edge of the roof. He was a long way up – much too high to jump. If he had been wearing his high-tech shoes and gloves, he could have crawled down the wall like a sure-footed beetle. That way, he might even have beaten Raven to the car park. But his gear with microscopic Velcro was in the XJ. He was trapped.

He couldn't even ram her car with his own because he needed a working BCI to operate the Jaguar remotely.

As he looked around for inspiration, he updated Angel on his mobile.

"Okay," Angel said. "I'll get on to air traffic control and find out if they've got any rogue aircraft. You get after her, Jordan."

"Easier said than…" He stopped talking as he stared at the flagpole. "I'm onto it." He put the phone away and grabbed the rope. Hauling on it with his left hand, he lowered the flag and uncoupled the rope from the pulley. Hoping that it was long enough, he forced the thick rope past the rigid thumb into his clenched right fist. Then he yanked on it. Luckily, it slid through the fingers. Perhaps it was even threaded too freely. But he didn't have a choice. His couldn't tighten the grip because the motors in his fingers weren't working.

He made sure one end of the rope was well anchored to the flagpole and then he laid it out to the front edge of the building. He looked down again. It was a long drop to the tarmac path. Heights had never bothered him, but falling was a different matter. He threw the rest of the rope over the edge and watched it dangling. He couldn't see clearly where it ended, but he was sure it hadn't reached the tarmac below. He hoped it was close enough. He also hoped that his lame false hand would provide the brake he needed if he wasn't going to die when he hit the ground.

His shoulders rose and fell as he took a deep breath. Then he jumped off the roof and the rope ran through his fist.

24 OVERRIDE UNSUCCESSFUL

There was no longer anything solid beneath his feet. Rushing through his artificial fingers, the rope yanked his disabled arm up above his head. But there wasn't enough friction between his fist and the rope so he plummeted down at breathtaking speed.

He'd never been abseiling, but this had to be similar. Without any of the safety features. And without the style. He had much more bravery than expertise. Swinging inwards, he crunched into the brick wall, bruising his back and legs.

Below him, Raven's car accelerated down the narrow lane towards the main road.

He was falling far too fast. The tarmac seemed to be zooming up at him alarmingly. At this pace, he knew he'd break both legs when he hit the ground. To increase the resistance between his false fingers and the threads of the rope, he twisted his whole body so the rope had to zigzag through his unresponsive fist. At once, even his disabled sense of smell detected the burning of synthetic skin, but he had no sensation of the heat. At least he was slowing.

As he neared the ground, the rope sliced into his artificial skin, shedding strips of silicone from his palm. Then, suddenly, he fell free of the rope and his right arm collapsed against his side. He hit the tarmac.

He felt the jolt first in his ankles, knees and hips. The shock wave flew up the rest of his body to his neck like an earth tremor, but the pain was confined to his legs as he crumpled onto the ground with a grunt.

He didn't have time to worry about the stinging sensation. He got to his feet and looked around. His Jag was right in front of him, but he couldn't use it. He couldn't transmit the codes he needed to operate it. But he had another idea. He limped towards the factory. Through the large window, he could see two huge diggers and a dumper truck.

Without a functioning right arm, he couldn't smash his way through the window or the main door, so he staggered to the back door that Raven had forced open. Trying to ignore the aches in his knees, he dashed across the lower floor and hauled himself up into the earth mover closest to the window. The key was in the ignition. He turned it on straight away and the giant vehicle burst noisily to life. He rammed the digger into first gear and the monster leaped forward. Jordan had hardly worked out where the controls were before it crashed through the window. Like icicles falling from a thawing gutter, shards of glass fell all around him. Jordan protected his head and face with his left arm and the digger lurched to the right.

Clear of the broken glass, Jordan steered the earth mover away from his Jaguar. He shifted the gear stick and the engine spluttered and groaned.

In front of him, Raven was reversing her stolen car crazily back down the narrow lane. Another car was forcing her back towards the car park. It had to be Kate in a white Toyota.

At once, Jordan saw what he had to do. He accelerated towards the lane to block off Raven's retreat. But the earth mover was nowhere near as nimble as his Jaguar. It seemed to take an age to turn and gather speed.

Shaking Jordan in its rough seat, the digger lumbered across the car park just in time. He brought it to a shuddering halt at the end of the lane.

Raven executed an emergency stop and skidded. The rear of her car smacked into the earth mover.

It was as if a dog had run into an elephant. In the driver's cab, Jordan did not feel a thing.

Kate turned and braked, stopping the Toyota across the width of the lane. Together, she and Jordan had boxed in Raven.

Laptop in hand, Raven got out and ran for it. She dashed away from the digger and the factory, but Kate was too quick for her. Drawing back her right arm, Kate punched Raven full in the face. Stunned, she came to a dead halt as if she'd run into an unseen plate of glass. Then her look of surprise changed to one of pain and her legs gave way. The laptop flew from her grasp as she fell to the ground.

Jordan winced at the power of the punch. Clambering down from the digger, he called out, "Ouch. Remind me not to get on your wrong side."

Kate smiled. "I've done a bit of boxing in my time. Hey, you look rough."

Jordan pointed to his false arm and then his head. "I'm out of action. Again."

Kate had brought help in the shape of Eli Kennington. Climbing out of the passenger door, he looked surprised, shocked and a little amused.

On the ground, Raven stirred and moaned.

"End of mission," Kate declared.

Remembering the two aeroplanes that Raven had sabotaged, Jordan shook his head. "Not really." He reached down for the laptop and said to Eli, "I need you to save a lot of lives. We don't have long." He began a hurried explanation.

Surprising all three of them, Raven came round from the blow. She jumped up and ran in the direction of the airport.

Taking a breath, Kate said, "You deal with things here. I'll get her." She set off in pursuit.

Jordan balanced the computer on the bonnet of Kate's car. "I'll make sure you get full access to all my gadgets if you stop some hardware Trojans that are going to bring two flights down any second now."

Eli jerked his thumb in Kate's direction. "She has already promised me that."

"Must be true, then."

Eli was about to say something else but he stopped, opened up the laptop and turned it on. Almost immediately, he muttered, "I'm blocked from using it.

It is protected by a password."

"Hang on. I've got an idea." Jordan called Angel and hurriedly filled him in on events. "What was Raven's name before she was Madison Flint?" he asked.

"Julie Baker."

"Okay." He turned to Eli and said, "Try Baker, Julie or Julie Baker – all one word or with a gap. Something like that. Hurry."

At the second attempt, the laptop accepted *juliebaker* as a password. "All right," Eli said, "I am past security." Seeing an icon for the program 'UnTrojan', he cried, "She stole this stuff from me!"

"Good," Jordan replied. "That means you'll know how to use it."

The 09.00 flight from Gatwick to Atlanta had taken off without incident. The Boeing 767 had 304 passengers on board. But the air traffic controller in charge of the departure was staring at her screen in amazement and horror.

Trying to remain calm, she said into her microphone, "Flight AM5699. You have deviated from your flight path. Please correct at once."

"Investigating," the pilot replied.

There was silence for thirty-two seconds. Then the pilot's voice told her, "The autopilot's in control of this aeroplane and all my attempts to override it have failed."

Control gulped. She could hardly believe her ears. "Say again."

"Override unsuccessful. I have no control over flight. The autopilot is flying the aeroplane. I don't know where we're going. Bearing north and descending steadily."

Further along the row of computers, another controller was having almost exactly the same astonishing conversation with Flight TOM4762 to Larnaca. The only certainty was that the Boeing 757 carrying 214 passengers was not headed for Cyprus.

25 SUDDEN DEATH

"Right," Angel said into Jordan's ear. "It's started. There are two rogue flights out of Gatwick. I've scrambled Air Force fighter jets with missiles primed and ready to fire."

Jordan didn't know that his boss wielded such power. Unit Red was a secret organization, but it had authority and contacts in high places.

"Where are they going?"

"At the moment, I'm waiting to see. Find a way to give

control back to the pilots or I'll have to blast them out of the sky."

Shocked, Jordan replied, "Eli's working on it."

"There are 518 people on those two planes, Jordan."

He swallowed. 518 lives in the hands of an autistic computer geek and a teenager with a broken body. "How long do you need?" he asked Eli.

"I am trying to determine what has been sabotaged. I can see that you..."

Jordan interrupted. "Don't worry about me. Look for planes."

"Yes. She has reprogrammed an American flight called AM5699."

"Well, unprogram it," Jordan almost shouted.

Eli typed as he replied, "It is possible, but it will take me a few minutes."

The phone still clamped to his ear, Jordan fell silent, allowing Eli to concentrate.

Before long, though, Angel said, "I think you were right."

"Oh?"

"They look like they're heading for Sizewell. If that's the target, I can't let them strike."

An image of a mushroom cloud sprang into Jordan's

mind. He shuddered at the thought of a nuclear explosion in East Anglia. He shuddered at the thought of the devastation it would cause. "How long have we got?" he asked, his voice suddenly quaking.

"A couple of minutes before I have to give the order to fire and destroy the planes."

Jordan turned to Eli. "Can you sort it out in two minutes?"

"No," Eli answered. "But I am making progress in releasing the first aeroplane's flight and control system."

"Flight AM5699," the air traffic controller said. "I'm told someone's trying to disable your autopilot remotely. Keep trying to override it. Repeat. Keep trying to regain control and prepare to alter course."

"We are flying at an altitude of five hundred metres, Control. Five hundred metres! Towards coastal buildings."

"I've got you on screen."

The pilot said, "I can see another commercial plane. I estimate on a collision course. I don't know if I'll hit the ground first or the other Boeing."

"We're doing all we can, AM5699. If you get

navigation back, fly east. Repeat. Go east over the sea. Flight TOM4762 has instructions to break away to the west, over land. Do you copy?"

"Copy. I note we have military escorts as well."

"Confirmed," Control said.

"What are *their* instructions?"

The air traffic controller hesitated. "The Air Force can't stand by if you're going to hit a sensitive target."

"Like Sizewell B? That's what it is, isn't it?"

There was another short period of radio silence before she answered. "Yes, confirmed. I'm sorry, AM5699."

Giorgos didn't know it but he was the youngest passenger on Flight TOM4762. In a cheerful mood, he and his family were taking up two rows of seats in the aeroplane. They were cheerful for two reasons. They'd seen Giorgos's cousin marry a nice English man in Oxford and now they were going home to Cyprus. Giorgos was smiling because he was remembering the English rain drenching the wedding party after the ceremony and his mum drinking too much at the reception. She was always funny when she'd had a few drinks.

The plane banked sharply to the right. Instead of continuing its climb into the grey sky, it lurched and began to descend. Giorgos noticed his mum exchanging a glance with the other adults. She was more surprised than scared.

As the aeroplane turned towards the coast and continued to descend, the grown-ups looked less puzzled and more panicked. With a strange feeling in his stomach, Giorgos gazed out of the window. The undercarriage almost seemed to be scraping the flat farmlands of the Suffolk countryside. He didn't know much about flying, but he knew the ground shouldn't be so close and he could sense everyone's nervousness.

Forcing a smile, his mother leaned close and spoke in English. "Everything's going to be all right. You'll see."

Pointing out of the window, he replied, "I see two more planes."

One was flying low, just like their own. The other was much smaller and higher. A jet like the ones in war films.

There was a hurried announcement in English that Giorgos didn't quite catch, but the look of horror on his mum's face told him they were in trouble.

"Right," she said to him, struggling to hold back tears. "We've got to get into the brace position."

"What's that?"

"Like this," she said, bending over so her forehead

rested against the seat in front. She also cradled her head in her arms.

"Why?"

"Because...the stewardess said so. Because we're too near the ground."

"But you said it'd be all right."

"Let's get you into the right position, love, then it will be."

Eli tapped at the keypad and then looked up. "That's it! I have freed the first system."

On the Suffolk coast, unseen by Jordan and Eli, the aeroplane bound for Atlanta peeled away from the coast under the control of its pilot and zoomed out over the North Sea. It almost skimmed the waves. But it was safe and it climbed back into the sky.

"One more," Angel said to Jordan urgently. "Flight TOM4762."

"TOM4762 as well," he roared at Eli.

"I know."

Chilling Jordan, Angel said, "You've got thirty seconds before I give the order to fire."

"Thirty seconds," Jordan told Eli. "Any hope?"

"None at all."

"There's got to be something..."

Eli shook his head. "With hurrying come mistakes."

"We need more time," Jordan said into the phone.

"There isn't any," Angel replied abruptly.

Eli was working as quickly as he could: typing, shutting down systems, entering codes. But he was only human. He didn't stand a chance.

In a broken voice, Jordan said to his chief, "Sorry. We're too..."

Angel had broken off. He was giving orders to someone else.

On Flight TOM4762, Giorgos could not sit still in the brace position. Silently, he uncurled himself and sneaked a look outside. He saw the other big Boeing veer away over the sea. His aeroplane was keeping to its course, over fields, towards some buildings on the edge of the land. To Giorgos, it didn't look like an airport.

After a few more seconds, movement caught his eye. The fighter jet had fired a missile. Again, it was just like he'd seen in films. This time, though, the weapon wasn't hurtling towards some fictional enemy. It was coming directly at him. It was coming directly at a real plane full of innocent passengers.

They weren't in the brace position in case of an accident. It was in case of an attack.

Giorgos let out a gasp and he shouted at his mum. "Look!"

"Keep your head down," she muttered.

"No! Look!"

Their startled faces at the window saw the incoming rocket, horribly close. Elsewhere on the plane, some people were screaming. In an instant, Flight TOM4762 was no longer recognizable as an aeroplane. In a giant explosion, it became a flying fireball. Breaking into flaming fragments, it plummeted towards the coast, one hundred metres short of Sizewell nuclear power station.

Kate was panting when she returned. On her own. "She gave me the slip. Sorry."

"Oh, no!" Jordan had just lost 214 passengers. Now he'd lost Short Circuit as well. Talking to Eli Kennington, he said, "UnTrojan me now. Quickly. I'm not letting her get away. Not after what she's done."

"What has she done?" Kate asked. "You look.... shaken."

Shaken was hardly the word. He felt terrible. He felt like a failure. And he felt angry.

"A plane's just been shot down, all because of her. More than two hundred people."

Kate gazed for a while at the ground. Then, unable to make eye contact with Jordan, she looked out across the field where Raven had made her getaway. "I wish I'd hit her harder. She wouldn't have got up again."

Taking him by surprise, Jordan's fine sense of smell returned. At once, he detected aviation fuel again. "That's better," he said to Eli. Talking to Kate, he added, "Maybe she's nicked another car by now."

Kate shook her head. "She'll have worked out Angel's monitoring reports of stolen cars. More likely, she'll jump on a train."

"And go where?" Jordan asked. "She won't go home. She'll know agents will be waiting for her."

Kate sighed. "I don't know."

"I hope she hasn't got a plane ticket."

"She won't leave the country. She wants to ruin this one first."

"We've got her computer. My guess is she'll go where she can get another one." Jordan's robotic arm jerked stiffly into life. It came up level with his shoulder as if he were making some strange salute.

Eli laughed happily.

In an instant, Jordan reclaimed control over it. He

shook it, bent it at the elbow, flexed the wrist and made a fist. "Thanks."

"I will release your other features now," Eli said to him.

"Good."

Eli typed some more and the disconnected BCI in Jordan's head came to life. It felt as if someone had just switched on a wireless broadband router. He was no longer cut off from the web.

"Hey!" Eli cried. "Someone's trying to network with this laptop."

"Raven!" Jordan lifted his right arm and smashed it down on the computer. He shattered the keypad, crushed the hard drive and put a sizeable dent in the bonnet of the Toyota. "I bet she was trying to take a copy of the Trojan programs."

"And download them somewhere else so she could carry on," Kate added.

"Maybe she was successful," said Eli.

For a moment, Jordan stared at Eli. Then he said, "She can't be far away and she must be in front of a computer right now."

"A computer shop or an internet café?" Kate suggested.

"I know," Jordan replied. "I'm online. Searching. Yes!

There's an internet café at the airport. That's the nearest. South Terminal. Come on!" He looked at the digger and two cars blocking the Jaguar's way. "It'll be quicker to use your car, Kate."

They jumped into the Toyota and Kate put her foot down. In four minutes, she screeched to a halt outside the South Terminal and parked illegally right outside the entrance. Bewildered, Eli didn't move as the other two got out and dashed inside. Jordan glanced up and down the concourse. He hesitated only for a moment.

His GPS chip told him exactly where he was and an augmented reality site gave him directions to the internet café. It overlaid the information on his vision.

"This way," he called, sprinting to the right and wincing at the twinges in his ankles and knees.

There had not yet been an official announcement about the fate of Flight TOM4762. No one had been told that AM5699 was returning to the airport. Gatwick looked almost normal, except that the departure and arrivals boards were beginning to show a lot of delays. The only sign of an alert was the appearance of two heavily armed guards at every check-in desk.

Together, Jordan and Kate dodged passengers, their luggage and check-in queues. They hurtled past shops, car hire kiosks, foreign exchange booths and travel information desks. They dashed up the escalator to Gatwick Village. At the far end, they ran into the internet café. And Raven was not there.

Jordan took a breath and said, "She's been here."

"How do you know?"

He sniffed the air. "Her perfume." Straight away, he spun round and stared down the length of the hall.

"What now?" asked Kate.

"A man somewhere just shouted, 'That woman's swiped my laptop!'"

"Did he? I didn't hear…"

"Look!"

A middle-aged man was chasing Raven as she dashed for the stairs and exit. He didn't stand a chance of catching her.

But Jordan could not afford to let her get away. If she'd downloaded her Trojan programs onto a memory stick and snatched a working laptop, she'd need only a few minutes to install the software before she was back in business. Devastating business.

Jordan took off.

26 FLYING SPARKS

Raven raced down the stairs and along the concourse. She probably didn't realize that Jordan was not far behind. Further back, Kate ran as fast as she could, but she couldn't keep up with Jordan's pace.

Outside, Raven came to an abrupt halt and stared at Eli Kennington with an expression of surprise. He was standing beside a white Toyota, watching as a security officer attached a rope to its rear. The uniformed attendant was preparing to hoist it onto a pick-up truck and remove it as a security risk. The truck's engine idled as the winch reversed the car slowly up the ramp.

When Eli spotted Raven, there was a flicker of recognition in his eyes. For a moment, neither of them said anything to each other. Then Eli blurted out, "You stole..."

Raven wasn't going to start a conversation. She'd probably worked out that Kennington would not be on his own. No doubt guessing that Jordan and Kate were nearby, she took one look at the man operating the winch and made for him. He was concentrating on dealing with the illegally parked Toyota so he didn't see her until it was too late. With all her strength, she swung the laptop at him and the edge thwacked into the side of his head, just above his ear. Instantly, he was dazed and confused. Raven yanked him away from the controller, jumped into the cab and jabbed her foot down on the accelerator.

Emerging from the terminal's main entrance, Jordan took in the situation at once. He hurtled towards the wagon as it screeched away from the kerb, not quite piggybacking Kate's car. He couldn't run fast enough to draw alongside the cab. The best he could do was to reach the back. The ramp was grating on the tarmac, sending out sparks, and the front wheels of the Toyota were still on the road. Held only loosely by the rope, the car was swinging dangerously and unpredictably from side to side. Yet jumping on board was Jordan's sole chance of hanging on to Raven. If he got his timing wrong, though, he could easily trap a leg. If he waited too long, she'd accelerate away from him.

He dived at the rear of the wagon, scrabbling to get a grip. He put his back against the left-hand side and his right foot on the Toyota to stop it slamming into him. Then he edged up the gap towards the winch and the cab. At every twist and turn in the road, he was jolted and pummelled, but still he clambered gradually up the steep ramp.

The wagon left the airport grounds and gathered speed along a single-carriageway.

The floor of the truck levelled out at the top, so the rear of the Toyota was not as free to sway into him. He grabbed hold of a rail attached to the back of the cab. He was safer there, but he had no obvious way of getting to the driver. He wondered if he should simply wait until she stopped, but he was eager to complete his mission. He didn't want to give Raven any more opportunities to escape.

He climbed up the wall of the cab, resting his feet on the rail. He could see right over it now and the wind blasted his face as Raven tore along a minor road at high speed. His hair streamed out behind him and his jacket ballooned like a small sail. Instinct made him keep his head down as the truck went under a low bridge though there was ample clearance. Then he decided what he had to do.

Eleven days ago in an idle moment, Jordan had wondered whether he could punch his way through the roof of a car in an emergency. Now he had an emergency and he was about to find out. But instead of bursting out of a car, he was going to try to break in through the top of the cab.

Holding on with his left hand, he raised his artificial arm. Flaps of silicone skin, ripped by the rope, dangled from his hand. Summoning strength and determination, he jabbed downwards with the fist. The metallic roof bent inwards and a slight gash appeared at the bottom of the dent. The small slit was enough to give him hope. He lifted up his arm again.

The wagon skidded round a corner. A clear attempt to throw him off the roof. The whole vehicle lurched and Kate's car smacked into the side-wall.

Jordan gave up on the idea of a second punch and instead clung on tightly. It was like being on a flimsy raft tossed by huge waves.

Raven turned the steering wheel violently again,

veered into a field and accelerated. Bouncing across the farmland, she tried to shake the intruder down from his perch above her head.

Jordan's body lifted at one moment and then bashed down onto the top of the cab the next. It didn't get any easier when the wagon went up a small slope, took off and almost immediately crashed down onto a stony track. The Toyota yanked on the rope and the winch gave way a little. Even more sparks sprayed from the edge of the ramp as it clattered over the stones.

Deciding that, sooner or later, the wild fairground ride would get the better of him, Jordan changed his tactics. As quickly as he could, he slid off the cab and grabbed the winch to steady himself. In danger of being crushed by the swaying Toyota, he made his way round the back of the pick-up truck, grasping the side for stability. Slowly, he neared the front of Kate's car. Perilously close to the lip of the ramp and the rough track, he clutched the side with his left hand and ducked down. Almost immediately, the car swung at him and struck his head. He lost his grip and fell flat on the metallic ramp. He had no choice but to keep as low as possible so, when the car slithered from side to side, it would move right over him.

He tried to concentrate on the underneath of the Toyota. Lifting his head to look down the length of it, the exhaust system hit his face but at least he spotted what he needed. A large flat area near the rear was the bottom of the fuel tank. A tube led from it to the engine. Wasting no time, he grabbed the pipe with his bionic hand and wrenched it from its fixing near the engine block. At once, petrol began to flow out of the broken end and trickle down the ramp.

Jordan rolled over and came out between the front and rear wheels. Sparks were still flying where the edge of the ramp scraped over the stones. He stood up and clambered onto the side of the wagon. Desperate to jump clear, he muttered a curse. The pocket of his jacket had caught on a post. He had no time to disentangle it. He yanked on the jacket, ripping the leather. Then he leaped into the air and away from the wagon. He landed with a thud at the side of the track. His legs crashed down on stone, but his upper body was cushioned by grass. Even so, he grunted with the impact.

Back up on his knees, he watched the pick-up wagon bumping along the track. He hoped the jolting would encourage more petrol to spill. For several seconds, though, he thought his strategy had failed. A mass murderer was getting away and it was his fault. But the fuel needed time to run down the slope. It needed time to meet a flying spark.

A few more seconds passed. The truck was nearing a country lane. Soon, Raven would turn onto a proper road and put her foot down. Before she reached the junction, though, it happened. Nothing dramatic at first. An unstable yellow glow appeared at the back of the vehicle. The front end of the Toyota had caught fire. Silently, the flames followed the flow of fuel to the tank. The trickle down the ramp acted as a liquid fuse. Jordan held his breath.

There was a loud whoosh and Kate's car exploded.

The Toyota jumped briefly into the air and then crashed down again onto the truck, spilling fuel and engulfing it in greedy flames. The wagon came to a blazing halt. The sudden inferno stripped the exterior paint from both vehicles and quickly consumed the car's seats, carpets and plastic interiors. Anything flammable was going up in smoke.

A second blast and a huge roaring column of flame told Jordan that the fire had sneaked into the truck's own fuel supply. His finely tuned hearing also distinguished a terrible scream.

Jordan was not alone in watching the technician removing the skin – or what remained of it – from his right hand and beginning the diagnostics program.

Someone else was very keen to learn about the technology that lay underneath the damaged layer of silicone.

Jordan was distracted from the degloving and testing procedure. His mind was on other things. His mood was inconsistent. One moment, he was perky and pleased. The next, he was down. He'd neutralized Short Circuit, but he'd lost a lot of innocent people on the way. "If only I'd got to Gatwick quicker..." Talking to Angel, he said, "I want to see a list of everyone who died on that flight to Cyprus. Right now, they're just a number. 214."

Angel denied his request. "I'll give you a list of the 304 people you saved, if you like. They're real people as well, not just a big number."

"They'll name the dead online."

Nodding, Angel replied, "I'm sure they will. But there won't be a list of the ones on Flight AM5699 – who are living, thanks to you."

"And to Eli."

They both looked at Unit Red's newest recruit. Eli Kennington wasn't really interested in the people, living or dead. He was savouring the technology around him, like a kid with an excess of birthday presents. Right now, he was fixated by the automated testing of Jordan's robotic functions.

Eli Kennington had got to know too much about Jordan,

Kate and Unit Red. Angel had little choice but to bring him in to replace Raven. His expertise with computers was not in doubt. His dedication was not in doubt. His curiosity in Jordan's technology could be satisfied safely within Unit Red. And he was a loner. He was ideal.

Deciding that he'd go through the victims' names online, Jordan changed the subject. "What about Raven?"

"I've had words with the hospital," Angel answered. "They're certain she's not going to make it. Too badly injured."

Jordan was downhearted. Too many people had already died while he was on the case. 214 passengers on Flight TOM4762, Phil Lazenby, Victoria Truman and Justice Edward Jackson. Now, Raven would make 218. Before Jordan had been assigned to the Short Circuit investigation, there had been other victims. Paige Ottaway, Carlton Reed and a lot of other air passengers in Ecuador. Jordan shook his head and sighed. He couldn't now summon up much sympathy for Raven. Besides, if she were to live, she'd be an embarrassment to Unit Red.

"You did well," Angel told him. "Do you know how many she would've slaughtered if she'd set off a nuclear explosion in East Anglia?"

"No."

"Thousands. And she was planning more. She was planning chaos. It could've run to millions. But, no, civilization remains intact. Society carries on."

"Yeah." But those 218 who'd lost their lives on his watch nagged at Jordan. Somehow, they outweighed the anonymous and untold lives he'd saved.

"The diagnostics say you're fully fit for purpose," the technician announced.

Jordan nodded. What was the purpose of a fourteen-year-old boy? To explore. To push the boundaries. To discover his talents. To work out what to do with his life. To have fun. Jordan had bypassed most of that, of course. He'd sacrificed it. The purpose of his life was already clear. He protected the nation.

Looking up from a screen showing Jordan's enhancements, a delighted Eli said, "You see like an owl and smell like a dog."

At last Jordan managed a smile. "That's not very nice – telling me I smell like a dog."

Eli remained straight-faced. "My meaning was obvious. You can smell as well as a dog."

Jordan laughed quietly. Working with Unit Red's newest agent was going to be interesting.

MALCOLM ROSE ON THE SCIENCE BEHIND *JORDAN STRYKER*

When I want to come up with a new idea for a story, I usually look to science because scientists are always discovering and creating new things. Some exciting advances are bound to be just around the corner. For a few years, I have been keeping an eye on the coming bionic age. There are so many new developments I'm fascinated by: brain implants that give vision to the blind and hearing to the deaf, robotic limbs controlled entirely by the mind, touch-sensitive skin for artificial hands, designer DNA, power-enhancing drugs, developing replacement body parts through stem cells, terahertz technology, a bat-like echolocation device to help the blind, generating electricity from body movement, smart clothing, and drugs to wipe painful memories. It's clear that human re-engineering is under way.

Some of these body enhancements are already hitting the news. When soldiers return from war zones with dreadful injuries – often missing a limb after an encounter with a bomb – their medical treatment can grab the headlines. In writing the Jordan Stryker thriller series, I've been inspired not only by what modern medicine and technology can do for people, but also by their determination to cope.

I have seen today's artificial arms in action. By the power of thought alone, they can hold food, stir tea and pick up a small key. Whilst this cutting-edge science enables the disabled, it does not allow them to bust through doors like Jordan does with his bionic arm. In creating Jordan Stryker, I have not limited myself to today's exact medical technology. I have allowed myself to imagine where the science of body enhancement might take us in the next twenty years or so. By then, there will be some amazing developments. I've simply allowed Jordan to have the technology right now. I've also given him some of the grit shown by real-life victims of serious injury.

I haven't given Jordan the fantastic powers of a superhero. That would have been interesting and exciting, but not what I wanted to write about. When Jordan walks up a wall, it's because super-grip shoes are on the way to becoming practical, not because he's transforming into a superhero.

At least one expert thinks the first bionic eyes will be developed by 2020. Of all Jordan's abilities, I have peered into the future most with his artificial eyesight. I suspect that the power and range of his fictional vision will not become reality for many years.

Several scientists are already talking about a time when people will merge with machines. This would be called the singularity. I don't know whether it will happen or not, but I wonder if it is to be welcomed or feared. If a human being and a machine become a single thing at some point, the hybrid will probably be really smart and live for ever. This seems too fanciful for Jordan, but he's certainly a step on the way to this awesome and unsettling future.

ABOUT THE AUTHOR

Malcolm Rose was born in Coventry and began his career as a research scientist. He started writing stories while studying for his DPhil degree in chemistry, as a means of escape from everyday life. He is now a full-time writer best known for his gripping science-based thrillers and forensic crime series. He has been awarded the Angus Book Award twice and the Lancashire Children's Book of the Year. His novel, *Kiss of Death*, was chosen for the national Booked Up reading scheme, and was shortlisted for four prizes, including the Salisbury Schools' Book Award.

For more information about Malcolm Rose visit his website: www.malcolmrose.co.uk

To find out more about the Jordan Stryker series visit: www.usborne.com/jordanstryker

Don't miss out on
JORDAN STRYKER'S
gripping First mission:

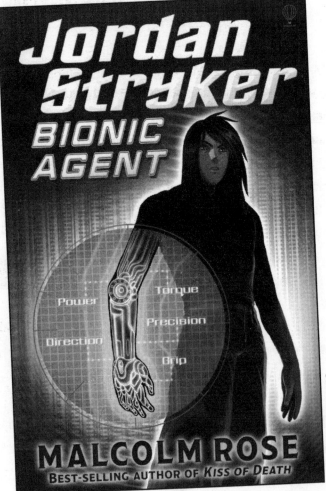

ISBN 9781409509752

A massive explosion destroys the south-east
of England. The near lifeless body of Ben Smith
is plucked from the carnage...

Deep within the secret headquarters of the
mysterious government agency, Unit Red, Smith is
rebuilt as...Jordan Stryker. New technology gives him
unbelievable new powers, and now he has a mission:
to hunt down the perpetrators of one of the biggest
crimes ever known.

Can Jordan outwit the evil masterminds and
violent gangs who will use any means to destroy
their enemies?

**"Buzzing with the thrills and spills of a James Bond
blockbuster..."**
Lancashire Evening Post

www.usborne.com/jordanstryker

Also by MALCOLM ROSE

FORBIDDEN ISLAND

Mike and his friends ignore the clear warning sign on
the island and decide to explore, not knowing just how
dangerous it will turn out to be. As they stumble across
a deadly secret, they realize they are alone in a race
against time...before they become the island's
next victims.

Enter a world of conspiracy and cover-ups in
this brilliant mystery.

**"A complex and chilling thriller...this pacy read asks
uncomfortable questions."**
The Daily Mail

ISBN 9780746098639

KISS OF DEATH

On a school trip to the plague village of Eyam,
Seth is moved by the story of how villagers sacrificed
their lives to the Black Death. Kim and Wes are more
interested in what they see at the bottom of the
wishing well – money!

But when they snatch the coins they also pick up
something they hadn't bargained for, and as the hideous
consequences of their theft catch up with them all,
Seth is forced to face a terrifying truth. Has Eyam's
plague-ridden past resurfaced to seek revenge?

**"Fast-paced, full of nail-biting moments and more than
one shock – not for the squeamish."**
Primary Times

ISBN 9780746070642

A. G. TAYLOR

METEORITE STRIKE

A meteorite has struck earth without warning,
unleashing a deadly alien virus. Thousands fall
victim...but not Sarah and Robert.

Instead they develop strange side effects – psychic
abilities. And that makes them a target for HIDRA,
a rogue international agency determined to turn them
into lab rats, just like the other kids they've already
captured – kids who can control fire, create storms
and tear steel with their minds.

If they can work together, these kids might
stand a chance against HIDRA...

SHORTLISTED FOR THE
WATERSTONE'S CHILDREN'S BOOK PRIZE

ISBN 9781409508571

ALIEN STORM

A freak virus released by a meteorite storm has given
Sarah, Robert and their friends amazing superpowers.
But such powers are both a blessing and a curse...

Deadly meteorites are heading to earth, but mysterious
Russian billionaire Nikolai Makarov seems gleeful.
What is his secret and can the group of friends
thwart his master plan?

A thrilling action-filled sequel to A. G. Taylor's
highly-acclaimed debut *Meteorite Strike*.

**"Takes the reader on a nerve-wracking ride filled
with...more moments of nail-biting tension than you
will find in many a Hollywood action film..."**
bookzone4boys.blogspot.com

ISBN 9781409520184

For more thrilling adventures,
check out
www.fiction.usborne.com